Invoking Destiny

Wands, Wings, and Wardens Series
Book 1

Invoking Destiny

EDITED BY ISABELLE REYNOLDS

STORIES BY:
I MICHAEL STANIFORTH I PAT O'MALLEY I ROXANA NEGUT I
I C. W. STEVENSON I SERGIO PALUMBO I SEATON KAY-SMITH I CATHY KIRK I
I PATRÍCIA SÁ I KAY HANIFEN I VALERIE WILLIS I

Dedication

To the entire 4 Horsemen Publications team for your constant support and encouragement

Table of Contents

Introduction

Magic and fantastical creatures have always been an interest for humans. We make stories to teach children lessons or to warn people away from certain areas of the ocean. Maybe even to help explain the unexplainable. We create creatures that we wish were real. Even though those same creatures would probably be major threats to humanity, it is still entertaining for us to imagine a world in which they exist.

We would love to be the heroes of these fantastical stories. I mean, who doesn't want to sacrifice themselves by being melted into a city wall to protect the inhabitants from demonic creatures? Wait. That sounds terrible. Maybe that is a bad example...

How about entering into a fairy's garden that is spelled to prevent you from reaching the coveted apple tree by impaling you with thorns in a maze made of sweet-smelling rosebushes? Huh. That one also sounds painful.

Let's try again.

A small band of border protectors investigates a series of gruesome murders in a forest in the dead of winter, but they find that the culprits are more than any of them are willing to risk their lives handling. Hmm. That also doesn't sound like the best set of circumstances.

So maybe we don't want to be the heroes of *those* stories. But they sure are fun to read.

But there are other situations in these pages that may sound more appealing to the average person. Such as being raised by a motherly dragon in the mountains with a small village nearby and plenty of company. Or maybe you can go fishing and catch a nice gift for your loved one. Sometimes asking the void for help with your magic means you get a cute little bunny rabbit that can talk and do your bidding. Just ignore its sharp teeth; we're pretty sure it's harmless.

You can find a nice place to rest in the mountains after a long walk and enjoy the view with a friendly spirit. You can live a provincial life as the Queen's favorite florist with a sweetheart you are planning on marrying soon. You can sail the ocean wide with your friends and family in order to make alliances with the neighboring villages, and maybe you make a stop on a tropical island along the way. You could even gain immortality to travel the world and enjoy the beauty of all creatures and civilizations.

You can do anything you want to inside the pages of a fantasy story. So, enter the realm of dragons, magic, knights, and fairies to live out your dreams. Or maybe just read about others living those dreams. Some of them may turn out to be nightmares.

In the Garden of Erolkin
by Michael Staniforth

A three-foot storm of chaos and sticky fingers descended upon Frida's home, far too soon after the first rays of the morning sun for her liking. Children, to her experience, existed exponentially. One was one and that was fine, but two were more like four, and three might as well have been ten. There were five in her home presently, and it was not a large place. She sighed as dust and hay whipped around the cyclone of little bodies before her. *At least they were occupied*, Frida thought to herself.

The children were fashioning their offerings, laid outside of their homes at the height of winter as a humble request for spring to come soon. Wicker effigies of what Frida presumed to be horses—or maybe pigs, it was hard to tell—were surrounded by offerings of food and stick figure images of a more verdant land than the snow-covered mud outside promised. The children were in Frida's house because she was old; old enough to know the stories, old enough to know the traditions and their origins by heart. And the village thought it would do her good, the crazy old spinster on the outskirts of life, to have their energy tear her home to pieces. In truth, for Frida, it did.

"Nana Frida?" one particularly rambunctious six-year-old girl asked. "Why do we make the offering?"

Nana was an honorary title, as Frida had no children of her own, let alone grandchildren, but it was one she took with pride, though she would never show it. The child knew the answer to her question, but she wanted to hear the tale, and that suited Frida, who wanted to tell it, just fine.

"Settle down!" she called to the storm, and it obeyed. "Settle down and I shall tell you all a story."

In the middle of the wood on the edge of the village, there lies a maze that cannot be solved, which leads to a gate of silver that cannot be opened, behind which lies a garden that cannot be seen: the garden of the Elf King, Erolkin.

Erolkin loves the winter. He loves the bite of the cold on his nose and toes, the crisp, clean air on a cloudless night, the hiding fogs of dusk and dawn, the sugar coating of frozen morning dew. He loves the bright reds and whites of the winter berries and the sharp cutting edges of the evergreen leaves. Winter is Erolkin's favorite time of year for all these reasons, but for one more besides, and above, all the others. Winter is a time of magic, a time when the barrier between his world and the world of Man is at its thinnest, and the doorway to his garden is open to the mortal realm: winter is the harvest time for Erolkin.

Erolkin's garden would be an imposing site to anyone who made it inside the large silver gates, ornate with metal flowers and vines, bees and ladybirds. Around the broad, heptagonal perimeter stands a border of tall spruce, straight and proud, and in the winter, the green needles spike out from underneath the snow in a display of their immutable life. The rosebush maze leading to the gates is, underneath the winter sheets, a gauntlet of dry, icy sticks and thorns. Under the warm rays of the summer sun, the scent of roses on the outside of the silver gates blends pleasantly with the lavender that blooms beyond. But the winter winds blow clean the stems of the *rosoideae* and the *nepetoideae*, allowing the more savory scents of thyme and sage— evergreen and ever present—to come through.

In winter, the floral nose of summer is preserved only in Erolkin's perfume, great tubs of which he swans about in; rose oil every morning to bring his loves to his garden for the day and lavender every night to bring them again in his dreams. Each night, Erolkin crows loud into the sky, calling his hundred children to him. Flitting through the leaves and moon beams, they gather the herbs and burn them at two small stone altars adorned with sliver wreaths of winter blooms, filling the Garden with their earthy smells. The smoke of those fires brings happy memories of times gone by to Erolkin as he cranes over them to swallow deep lungfuls of his enchanted past.

Upon Erolkin's radiant brow sits a wreath of bay laurel, a crown for a king. His little bay tree forest suffers so in the deep cold of winter, but the crown connects his spirit and that of the forest, and so long as both are living, both will thrive in any weather, through any storm. Not so endangered though are his forests of cedar and pine, which are strong and prosperous all the year round, just like Erolkin himself; the wealthy king of the woods who has all of nature's bounty at his disposal. Around his neck, Erolkin bears a cone each of the cedar and the pine, and with these tokens he is free to raven his garden, as well as any mortal wood, at his will.

These are the flora of Erolkin's garden, the secrets of his magic and the source of his power, which are with him at all times: the rose and the lavender on his flesh, the sage and the thyme in his lungs, the cedar and the pine around his neck, and the bay laurel upon his head. These natural gifts drive mortal men to jealousy, but it is at the center of his garden that lies the prize which sends those men to their deaths. For at the very focal point of his domain, equidistant from each apex of the seven-pointed star, drawing ancient and arcane energies from each of Erolkin's gifts, stands an apple tree which boasts a single perfect fruit: a smooth, silver-skinned apple with golden flesh. A single bite from this wondrous fruit, so the stories tell, will bestow on a mortal person all the gifts of Erolkin and his kingdom besides. It is the seat of his power, the distillation of his will, and it is this that tempts so many to risk death for eternal life, at the height of winter's shortest day, when night's magic opens Erolkin's garden to the world.

One midwinter night, cold and dark and full of magic, Erolkin larked about in the sky, high above his pristine Garden, admiring its snow-white blanket which softened the edges of his world to cotton. That night, at the height of the moon—which is never so high as the trees in the garden—a ghostly, evanescent light was cast on his world, illuminating the path for one unwary hero who would taste Erolkin's apple for herself.

Erolkin's ears pricked, and, eagle-eyed, he gandered at his prey who fought her way through his rosebush maze. Erolkin hawked down upon his quarry from the skies, and at the last moment before being spotted, he ferreted himself amongst the rosebushes to conceal himself from the hero's watchful eyes. He snaked his way down to the ground through the branches and bark, but Erolkin has the protection of the cedar and the pine, and so he was not cut by the thorns that might nick at his skin. Upon reaching the garden floor, he wormed away under the snow so as not to disturb its pristine coating and give himself away. He wanted to watch the sport, he wanted to savor the attempt and the folly of this adventurer.

This mortal hero wore shining armor of pure iron; heavy, inflexible, and foolish. She needed no protection from Erolkin, for he was quite content to observe from the undergrowth, and she would have been better served by warmth and the freedom to move swiftly. She might have hoped at least for protection from the roses' thorns, but the branches of Erolkin's bushes are slender, and the gaps in the hero's armor were wide. Soon enough, her metal skin concealed one thousand tiny cuts that might have led a lesser person to death right there in the maze. Indeed, she struggled to keep her footing as she trod on along a path paved with the smooth, round skulls of her predecessors who had fallen at this first defense.

This hero had some wisdom about her, however. Thwarted at first by Erolkin's labyrinth, unable to find the true path, she held her arm out to the western wall, closed her eyes, and allowed the pinprick of the thorns to guide her. By this method, slowly but steadily, she eventually reached the end of Erolkin's maze and found herself face to face with the gateway to Erolkin's garden. The hero placed her iron gauntlets against the lock of the silver gates before her and pulled. Natural met supernatural, and the metal of the gate heated and popped until she could force open the gateway and enter Erolkin's garden.

The fumes of the burning sage and thyme immediately burst forth upon her, merged thick with the icy mist that hung in the winter air, and scorched the hero's lungs with a stabbing fusion of hot and cold. She hacked and retched, throwing her helmet to the ground and falling to her knees to take gulps of lower, cleaner air. But the herbs were already making their magic in her veins, and her head swam as the gases seeped into her blood. Hounding his prey from the shadows, Erolkin foxed the hero further with a spritz of his own perfume, lulling her into her dreams.

Opening her eyes now, the hero saw in those dreams her loves and her lovers from warmer times. She saw the faces of people she had lost years before, and desperately wanted to reach out and touch them, to embrace them to her bosom. The armor that she clung so tight to her breast, the shield on which she had bet her life, became a burden to her, a barrier between her and those she had lost and left behind. Reaching up, she unclasped both her breastplate and backplate, cast off the heavy metal carapace, and rose to her feet to run to her family and friends. She progressed four, maybe five, steps before her legs buckled and she tumbled back to her knees, her limbs weak and shaking. Her face sank into the snow, and the ice cut coldness into her flesh and shook her from her fantasia. The images of her loved ones scattered on the wind and the hero awoke to find herself once more in the garden, now without her armor, exposed to the elements, her legs quivering, and her fingers numb from the cold.

The armor was lost and left behind, its crest as fallen as the snow. To turn back even one step would mean death to the hero. Moving forward and the sweet flesh of the silver apple were her only chances for survival now. Forcing herself to her feet, the hero pushed her mortal legs one step after another deep into the wooded regions of Erolkin's garden. She moved slowly through the bay trees, fighting against the cold and growing weaker with every step. Her heart beating in her chest began to slow, and she felt the creeping fingers of death clutching at her shoulders, trying to drag her down into the underworld beneath the dirt at her feet, down to the devouring worms. Fear began to well up inside of her; fear of death, fear of eternal torment, but most of all, fear of her own failure, that she might fall here without tasting of that revitalizing fruit. The hero dove down into this fear. She embraced it, felt every drop of it pumping adrenaline through her system. Using the power of her fear, she forced her heart to pick up its natural pace once more, and she moved in step with it, one foot forward for one beat.

A forest of pine trees now stretched away from the hero in every direction. She could not say how or when she had come to be surrounded by this woodland, nor could she see through the dense trunks about her to a path, a direction, or an ending. Her world had become a kaleidoscope of repeating greens and browns, fractal, endless, unfathomable. With no wall to follow and no thread to pull, she stopped dead in her tracks, unsure of where to head next. The hero closed her eyes and stood for a moment, shaking in the cold. She could not trust her senses in this realm. They would play tricks, or tricks would be played on them. She must keep moving or she would perish from exposure, but she could not look ahead at a path she could not see. She closed her eyes tight, breathed the scent of the path before her and walked steadily forward, trusting in her idea of the road more than the fact of it, seeing beyond her sight. This way she made headway, slow but continuous, and though her strength continued to wane, her courage did not as each step became more an act of will than of muscle. Cowed at the cleverness and determination of this intruder unlike any that had come before, Erolkin beetled ahead of the mortal woman to watch her fall into his final trap.

The truth about the Fay Folk is that they do not play fair, and they do not leave things to chance, no matter what the stories may say. So, to call the cedar woods of Erolkin's garden a trial to mortal heroes would be unjust. Without the protections with which Erolkin covers himself, no mortal could ever have the strength to break through the barrier that the cedar wood forms and come out into the orchard beyond to find the silver fruit. Thus, though the hero was valiant to reach it, and though she gathered unknown strengths to push hard against it, the magics which protect the center of Erolkin's garden pushed back harder, crushing against her, snapping her bones, and splitting her muscles. She was the strongest of her kingdom, perhaps of her world, and Erolkin turtled into the trunk of the apple tree, amazed, even impressed, as she forced against his magic. She could not break through, and yet she pushed on, the barrier could not break under mortal hands, and yet it strained. The hero strained back, her arms turned to steel, her mind gained the resolve of a falling stone, and with a final impossible effort, the branches of the cedar wood gave, and she fell into the clearing of the apple tree. Yet as she broke through the barrier, it too broke through her. A branch of cedar pressed against her breast as she had pushed against the trees, and a fragment of it forced its way through her tunic and into her heart.

The damage to the hero's body was fatal. The only thing that could save her was the glistening silver fruit, so tantalizingly close to her grasp. She rose on what was left of herself, half her full height, a tenth her full strength, a fraction of her mortal life left within her. Each step she took brought her closer to the earth at her feet. Each inch she moved forward was an inch she fell down. Finally, all life within her spent, all hope within her gone, she succumbed to the cold and to mortality as she collapsed beneath the bough of the apple tree. As she fell, she stretched out her hand in one last desperate clutch at her prize. Her fingers dusted the surface of the apple, so close to the end, the closest that any mortal had ever come. Yet despite all her efforts, there in the snow, she died.

Erolkin weaseled up the hero's corpse and onto her outstretched hand. Shrewd as the forest he protected, he brushed a smudge of silver from the tips of the hero's blue-white fingers, as stiff as branches from the cold and growing stiffer with encroaching decay. Erolkin rid the branch of its apple, and using moss and snow to sponge away the silvery paint, he revealed the healthy, natural, green skin beneath. Greedily, Erolkin wolfed down the succulent flesh—which was white and not gold—of the wholly unmagical fruit: perfectly normal, perfectly natural, perfectly delicious. Replete, he gave a contented grin to himself and to the corpse beneath him. Fairies leave nothing to chance.

The faces that stared up at Frida were hovering on the edge of wailing. It was a cruel story, but it was an important one. One that needed to have an impact with the children. The girl who had instigated the whole experience with her questions clearly had not yet learned enough and screwed up her mouth with a forming question, bitter on her tongue.

"Why did he have to kill her?" the girl asked.

Frida smiled down at the child.

"He didn't kill her," she said, allowing a bit of hope to shine through the children's gloom, and then snatching it away before it softened them too much. "Her greed is what killed her," Frida said, and their drying tears sprang forth again. "She thought she could take whatever she wanted and give nothing back, but that's not how the world works, that's not how nature works. Everything has its price, and that's why we leave our gifts for the Fay Folk, so that we might take the fruits from the forests and the earth, which belong to them and not us."

The children's ferocity dispelled, the storm of young feet and fingers dispersed and blew them back to their respective homes. On the way out, one particularly small boy, perhaps too small for such stories, held out a sweet to Frida which she recognized as having been purloined from her own pantry.

"You keep that and leave it out for Erolkin," Frida told the boy. "He likes sweet things almost as much as you do!"

The boy nodded and ran, and Frida closed up her home and began clearing up after the chaos. It was a hard story indeed, but in truth, not as dark as she made it out to be. She never told the children the whole story. Death was not truly the punishment that the hero received; it was life. She never told them of how the hero had awoken, outside the rosebush maze, her armor broken and useless beside her; of how the scrap of wood in her heart bound her by magic to Erolkin and had given her not death, but unnaturally long years, years in which she had watched so many generations come and go, so many friends live and die; of how the hero went to those silver gates with a bushel of apples every year for the Elf King, a tribute for her long life and a penance for her greed.

Frida went through to her back room where a rusty and beaten armor breastplate sat in the corner, neglected but never forgotten. She finished packaging up a bushel of the most delicious of her crop of apples for the year, took up her cloak and boots and set off into the midwinter night to leave her gift, and remember her story, which she would tell until the wood in her heart rotted to nothing and she could finally return with it to the earth.

The Audit

By Pat O'Malley

"Can I help who's next?" the bank teller asked.

A short, dark-skinned woman in her early thirties wearing a dark business suit walked up to the counter.

"Good morning. My name is Rubina Saanvi. I'm with the SEC. I think you've been expecting me." Rubina flashed her SEC ID badge to the teller.

Blood drained from the teller's face. He was a skinny man around her age, dressed in a dark suit and tie. He wore glasses in front of an oval-shaped head that had been shaved to ironically avoid looking like he was balding. The other bank tellers to the right of him looked on anxiously as if they too had been dreading this moment.

"Oh I... I'm sorry. Yes, you're right. We have been expecting you! Welcome to Sun Hammer Financial Center! My Gary is name. I mean my name is Gary! Sorry, I'm a bit of a spaz today. Long weekend!" He laughed anxiously.

"Nervous about something?" she asked.

"What? Nervous? Me!? I've never been calmer in my life! Come right this way I'll show you around and we can get this audit started."

The vaults of Sun Hammer Financial Center weren't anything too imaginative. They were typically the kind of metal vaults used by nearly every bank within and outside of the country. All along the corridor of the back office were giant chrome metal boxes that stored thousands of dollars, bonds, and stock shares.

"As you can see our vaults are composed of solid titanium steel and are very secure. So secure that there hasn't been a single attempted robbery in the entire history of Sun Hammer's operations," the teller informed, smiling proudly.

Rubina walked down the hallway, peering into each room, and gave each of the metal vaults a glance. Looking on, the teller appeared to relax as he watched the SEC agent smile and nod satisfactorily at each vault.

"Impressive display. I know that I wouldn't be worried if I stored my cash here," she said.

"I know, right? Hold on. You know what? I am such a spaz, I forgot I had something to give you!"

Spinning around, the teller beelined to an office at the end of the hallway. A moment later, the teller emerged holding a large manila folder in his hands. After running back down the hallway with an eager smile on his face, he handed the folder over to her.

"I understand that a large part of this audit is due to some inconsistencies made in our annual reports. Wouldn't you know, that lousy financial calculating software we installed still has some bugs in it? If you read this new report, you'll find that all of our receipts and finances have been corrected."

Flipping through the pages, Rubina skimmed through the new documents. To the best of her knowledge, the errors in the original report had indeed been remedied. Any financial advisor worth their degree would see the report and tell you that it was a lucid detailed account of the earnings of any successful bank. Unfortunately for Sun Hammer, she knew the horrifying truth. Closing the folder, she placed the document into her purse.

"Well then, perhaps my trip to the Catskills may have been for nothing," Rubina said, smiling.

"It's perfectly all right. Everyone here at Sun Hammer is always happy to cooperate with the SEC," the teller said.

"I'm happy to hear that. Let's see now, I have almost everything I need to mark this audit complete. I just need two more things then I can go on my way."

"Excellent! I have everything you need ready and available."

"Good, then first I would like to see the rest."

The teller's smile cracked. "The rest? I'm not sure I know what you mean."

"I think you do. In all fairness, you and the rest of the staff should be commended on the vaults; they do look authentic. Good for drawing attention away from the real valuables that are under our feet."

"I... I'm not following you."

"Do not patronize me, sir. If you want to make this audit disappear, you'll need to lead me to the rest of the money. Otherwise, I'll come back next week with a subpoena. It's your choice."

"W... wasn't there a second thing you wanted?" Gary was tugging at his tie, and he had begun to sweat.

"I'd like to have a word with your boss."

"Oh, did I not mention? I am the manager."

"Yes, I'm sure you all worked out quite the little arrangement. You or one of your coworkers play the face, handle the customers, and take home some golden coins, all while he pulls the strings from down below. My point is, we know Gary. Everyone at the SEC knows about what lies beneath this building."

There is a brief, but sublime, moment when someone's face changes to pure dread. When the listener hears the absolute worst thing they could hear, where all pretenses of decorum have been discarded, and all that's left is a vaguely human-shaped mask of primal fear. That mask was now on Gary, and it stared directly at Rubina.

"Y... you're crazy! I don't know what you're high on but I'm going to call and report you to the SEC!"

"Okay, I'll go. You'll be hearing from us soon. Enjoy telling your boss how well the audit went."

She walked towards the exit as if she was going to leave. She even made it so far as walking halfway through the hallway's entrance before a panicked voice called out to her.

"Wait!"

She turned around and met Gary's eyes with an expectant look on her face.

"Follow me." His voice had dried into a whisper.

As they walked past the vaults, the ominous sound of both of their expensive shoes tapping on the clean tile floors filled the air with each step. At the end of the hallway, they opened and walked through a small door. Inside was an otherwise average-looking office. The wall to the right was lined with bookcases, and straight ahead was a desk with a silver MacBook desktop computer resting on it.

The teller walked over behind the desk and reached for a thermostat on the wall. Flipping open the thermostat revealed an electric keypad, which the teller pressed a series of numbers into. By Rubina's count, the combination was over a dozen numbers long.

With a final beep, something behind the wall clicked, and with a grinding sound, the wall suddenly slid open, revealing an entrance. The pair were greeted by a gust of cold wind that blew out from the passageway. The change was surreal; only a moment ago there was just a blank wall. Now there was a doorway in this cluttered office, whose steps seemed to lead down into a dark sub-basement of the bank.

"It's pretty dark down there, we'll need these." The teller reached into the desk and pulled out a torch and matches.

"Shall we?" She extended her arm towards the howling abyss.

The teller looked on at the darkness anxiously; he seemed desperate for any excuse to stall.

"Ms. Saavni, Rubina, right? Look, we don't have to do this. Why don't we all just go on about our business? Please, for God's sake just submit those datasheets I gave you! I'm begging you, don't make me bring us to him."

"We can discuss all of this downstairs with your boss."

As she said this, a tremor of fear jolted her body. She had been claustrophobic and afraid of the dark all her life, but she knew exactly what she was getting herself into when she drove to the Catskills. Time was money, and she didn't have time to be afraid. Turning his fearful head towards the passageway, the teller gulped nervously as he lit the torch. The two entered the doorway and walked down the staircase.

Down into the dark.

As they journeyed into the underground, the amber glow of the torch revealed step after step, each one descending in a spiral. Occasionally, the teller would swing the torch irritably at some bats that came screeching out from the dark like one might shoo a fly. Rubina hardly noticed the bats; she had much bigger things on her mind.

After a long walk down the spiral staircase, the two had made it to the underground. Ahead of them was a dark tunnel that led towards a tiny pale-blue light in the distance. They followed the light until they eventually came upon its source.

"Aren't you coming?" She turned back looking at the teller.

"Oh um, w... well you said this is between you and our boss. I uh ... wouldn't want to get in the way of things, so I'll just be right here." The teller laughed anxiously.

"Very well, this shouldn't take long."

Taking a deep breath, Rubina stepped past the ancient runes and headed into the tunnel. Following a glittering light straight ahead, she walked further until she came upon a vast room where suddenly it wasn't so dark. There was no mistaking it: this was the room that she was looking for.

Standing alone, she stared in awe at a room whose size seemed to defy physics. Deep beneath the carpeted floors of Sun Hammer was a cavern the size of several football fields. An impossible cave of unexplainable beauty, the type of sight that you might glimpse only in dreams.

Treasure, shining, glittering treasure was everywhere. As far as the eye could see, there were gold, diamonds, and jewels piled on top of each other. It was like staring at dunes made out of hundreds of lottery jackpots. She was surrounded by priceless valuables that looked to come from all corners of the world.

There were opened pirate chests overflowing with golden coins, a golden sarcophagus of some forgotten pharaoh decorated with ancient rubies beneath a content golden face. Adjacent to the sarcophagus, an ancient golden sculpted ox stared on indifferently toward pyramids made entirely out of stacks of 100-dollar bills. Anyone coming within arm's reach of such a tempting sight could be forgiven for becoming mad with greed and racing to stuff their pockets in a frenzy.

Only once their pockets were full would they notice just how swelteringly hot it was inside the pit.

Rubina picked up a handful of golden coins from the pile closest to her. With a look of bemusement on her face, she let the golden circles rain from her hand, clattering back to the pile. In the corner of her eye, she also caught a look at the pile of charred human skulls and bones lying amongst the priceless valuables.

Slowly, from the depths of the enormous treasure cave came a grumble. That grumble quickly turned into a ferocious roar that rattled the earth and echoed through the cavern. Wincing, she covered her ears as the roar became an inhuman screeching scream. She prayed that the scream wouldn't burst her eardrums. It was the scream of a dark forbidden language that mankind was never meant to know.

Shifting in the darkness beyond the treasure, there came two golden slits that unfolded into thin black pupils that reminded her of feline eyes. Then, in a terrifying lunge, a giant reptilian head the size of a school bus shot out from the dark. Thundering with each step, the giant lizard with the obsidian scales covering its body stood out like a sinister, crawling shadow amongst the shining, colorful treasure. Sharp bronze spikes poked out from behind the creature's head and continuing to its back, acting as a divider for the two large, twitching leather wings that flexed in agitation.

Screeching still, the beast suddenly began to cough and make a choking sound as large fireballs shot out from its maw with each burst. To her mind's comprehension, it seemed to make a noise as though it were clearing its throat. Finally, it stopped, and those golden cat eyes turned towards the SEC agent.

"Sorry, morning breath." The towering monstrosity leered as flames billowed from its nostrils.

"In the eons before the universe took form, the old ones named me Yam-Nahar. In the time of man, they named me Brendicroit the Dark. Today, you may know me as the general manager of Sun Hammer Financial Center. How may I help you?" it said in a deep, gravelly voice that smelled like burning tar.

"Rubina Saanvi, I'm from the U.S. Securities and Exchange Commission, here in regard to an audit." She instinctively flashed her ID.

"Merlin's Tits. That was today? Where's Gary? Didn't he give you that new report?"

"Yes, the new report you had written up was excellent. You'd never guess what it was masking. Unfortunately, we've been tracking your actual records, and we've noticed huge discrepancies in your earnings and inventory. According to our reports, there is too little to show for the vast amount of riches that go into this bank. Also, keeping your bank's deposits haphazardly in a giant underground cave is generally frowned upon by the SEC."

"Oh dear, that sounds serious." It chuckled the way she always imagined the monster under her childhood bed did.

"Woman, perhaps I didn't make myself clear. I am Brendicroit, son of Jormungand, the Midgard Serpent who brought about the ancient gods' destruction at Ragnarök. Mankind only ever dared to leave your caves because I gave you the gift of fire! Despair, for I was the one who ate Beowulf!"

"That reminds me, we also have yet to see any qualification for you to manage a bank in the first place." She tried not to break eye contact as she slowly reached for something in her bag.

"Impossible! I took an online course!"

"You know that you're operating an illegal bank. The increase in business isn't just attracting treasure hunters. Now, normal, hard-working people are creating accounts with you and having their money tossed into a huge pile of gold."

"Hmmrph. I wouldn't expect you to understand. Any fool can go out searching for treasure like a drunken sea captain, but it takes real brains to have the treasure brought to *you*. Creating a bank as secure as Sun Hammer was the best thing to happen to the little people of this little town. What of it if a few dollars got lost in the tide? Nobody got hurt."

"Nobody?" she gestured towards the pile of charred human bones.

"Honestly, must I explain the joy that comes from telling an employee they're fired right before incinerating the flesh from their tiny bones?"

"I see. So, am I to understand that a factor in terminating your employees is a desire for puns?"

"Er ... yes?"

"Mhmm." She made a disapproving face as she jotted down something on her clipboard.

That hideous screeching roar returned.

"I don't need to listen to this! To hell with you and your audit! Now burn! Burn like all the others!"

Flapping its wings, the roaring mass of black scales and bronze spikes hissed a torrent of hellish fire. The flames were hotter than any flame known to man, and they were heading straight towards her. In a few seconds, she would join the pile of crispy human remains on the floor.

Or she would have if she didn't have the flute.

As she felt her eyebrows singe off, Rubina brought the ancient flute to her mouth. She ignored the taste of dust and tree bark and blew a single shrill note. The sound overpowered the roar of the fire as the penetrating sound of the flute rang in the treasure cavern like hell's teakettle. Once the flames reached her, they suddenly curved away from her, almost as if the creature's hell breath knew that it wasn't welcome.

"Wait ... what?" The fire-breathing lizard stared dumbfounded.

With her eyes closed, she continued to blow out the three single notes. It was the tune of "Hot Cross Buns," the only song she knew how to play on the recorder. The flute sounded severely out of tune, but it did its job. The ancient reptile's fire twisted and danced all around her, forming intricate shapes and patterns, but not once did they burn her. The soaring jet of fire swirled around her a few more times before combining into a large fireball above the sea of jewels and exploding into a powerful display of autumn-colored fireworks.

Given the monster's face, it might have been difficult to discern, but from where she stood, Rubina knew that for the second time today she was staring at a face wearing the look of unspeakable dread.

"Where... did you get..."

"Hold still and listen." She blew another note from the flute.

In a single spasm of muscles, the bronze-spiked body suddenly became frozen in place. Rigor mortis couldn't have done a better job. Like a predator caught in a trap, the creature hissed and struggled to move, but it was all in vain.

"The SEC has been around for a long time," she explained calmly as she lowered the legendary flute of H. R. Belphegor, The Dragon Tamer from her lips.

"Do you understand now Brendicroit? You were never going to escape the SEC. We know everything about you. I was sent here to hold you accountable, and I'm very good at my job." She tried to appear in control, but her hands were trembling, and her heart was pounding like a jackhammer.

"Release me woman or..."

"Rollover." She blew another shrill note.

"What? No! Damn you!"

The fire-breathing terror began rolling in the treasure beneath him. The pyramids made of 100-dollar bills were knocked over as he steamrolled over the treasure dunes. Golden coins and rubies were scattered everywhere.

"Enough," she said.

The giant reptile stopped mid-roll on its back and looked at with furious cat eyes.

"Do you finally know who is in charge now or do I need to put you on a leash and take you out for a walk?"

"Joke's on you. I'm into that."

Unamused, Rubina tore off a receipt of the audit from her clipboard and placed it on the ground.

"As of this moment, Sun Hammer is finished. I and everyone else at the SEC will sort through the valuables and refund your clients."

"Very well, I know when I'm beaten. Now, why don't you put the flute down as a symbol of friendship?"

"I have everything I need here. I'll leave you to close up." As she turned her back on the treasure pit and made towards the exit, she heard another roar.

"You think you're so clever? This isn't over!"

"It is Brendicroit. It's time for you to shut down your bank. Now get to it." She blew a final note into the flute.

"NOOOOOOOOOOOOOOOOOOO!"

With the sounds of hellish screeching and thrashing behind her, she held on to the flute and her bag for dear life and began running. With wisps of smoke still trailing off her frazzled hair and office clothes, she nearly crashed into Gary when she reached the tunnel's entrance.

"So, everything's okay then?" Gary asked as she raced past him.

"Run!" she yelled as she grabbed a torch hanging from a wall and sprinted back the way they had come.

Violent tremors shook the underground tunnel, the roof looking like it was beginning to crack. Any moment there could be a cave-in. Running in the dark, she could hear the sounds of Gary desperately trying to catch up to her. She was pleased to find she still had some luck left, as it wasn't hard finding her way out. She just had to follow the trail of frantic rats and bats racing to escape. Soon she found her way to the foot of the stone staircase.

With the frightened bank teller behind her, Rubina ran up the stairs as fast as she could. Just when she thought she could see the office-room light up ahead, a violent tremor caused her to stumble, but she caught herself before she could fall back downstairs to certain death.

"We're almost there! Hurry!" Rubina yelled, trying to keep herself steady as she raced up the staircase.

Debris fell from the ceiling, nearly crushing her as the rumbling grew increasingly more violent with each passing second. Finally, the duo made it to the top of the staircase and back into the office behind the vaults. Above ground wasn't much safer: there was pandemonium breaking out in the bank lobby.

A piece of the ceiling fell off and flattened an ATM in a shower of sparks and crushed metal. No one in the bank, much less Mooresville, was used to an earthquake, so there was mass confusion and hysteria as everyone tried to find safety. Everyone, customers and bank employees alike, stampeded out of Sun Hammer with Rubina and Gary trailing behind.

Outside, a large crowd had gathered. It seemed like everyone in Mooresville was drawn to the chaos like ants to a picnic. Everyone watched in awe as cracks grew all along the stone walls and red cobblestone roof. It was only after the last straggler made it outside that the bank began rocking back and forth. Then like a fragile glass statue, the beautiful stone building began to collapse.

One after the next, each of the bank's marble pillars broke and crumbled to the ground in a loud crash. People gasped as the golden chalice in the colorful stained-glass window shattered into a rainbow explosion of glass shards when the bank's roof caved in. All anyone could do was dodge the raining glass and watch as the mighty bank fell, leaving behind nothing but a mushroom cloud of dust. Once the dust settled, Rubina brushed herself off and walked to the front of the bank's ruins, trying to look professional.

"I imagine you all have some questions," she said.

"It's gone. It's all gone," Gary said in a disbelieving daze. One of the lenses of his glasses had popped out.

"I can imagine this is all very shocking, and I apologize for eradicating your jobs, but the SEC will ensure that Sun Hammer provides severance packages. Once we have a team recover everything from the pit, everyone with an account at Sun Hammer will be refunded in full."

As soon as she said that, a surging roar came from the crater.

In a fiery blaze, a wall of hellfire burst from the crater. Then just as suddenly, a gigantic fire-breathing lizard rocketed out from the flames like a demon from hell. People screamed and fled while others stood around in astonishment, taking photos on their phones. The winged nightmare was still yelling and cursing in a dark forbidden language as it soared off far away toward the cloudy mountains.

Getting her wits together, she tried not to throw up then and there. She had shut down Sun Hammer and delivered a warning to Brendicroit. Rubina would be feeling much more triumphant if not for the looming thought of everything she would have to include in her final report on the audit.

A moment ago, she had humiliated a creature older than humanity like it was nothing. Now she was anxious about some paperwork. Standing there amongst the horrified and awed crowd in her extra-crispy suit, near hyperventilating from the chaos of that morning, she was beginning to feel light-headed when suddenly she heard a voice.

"Jesus Christ, is that a fucking dragon?" someone yelled.

"Another audit completed," Rubina said, smiling to herself.

Brushing herself off, the SEC agent made her way through the frenzy of startled onlookers and walked towards the nearest bar. She could still hear the inhuman roar gradually growing fainter in the sky, but eventually she stopped paying attention.

The Story of the Little Goblin, Art, from the Iron Land

By Roxana Negut

Translated from Romanian by Andra Fundulea.

Once upon a time, there was a secret place on earth, well hidden from the eyes of men, and this place was called the Iron Land. It was a kingdom hidden between the darkest mountains and deepest chasms of the six kingdoms, surrounded by wild and dark forests, numerous caves and chasms, and inhabited entirely by goblins: hideous little creatures who shunned the gaze and company of other enchanted creatures.

In this fantasy land, things were not usual: here night was day and day was night for the little goblins. They slept by day in dark caves—because for many hundreds of years their eyes could not bear the strong glare of the sun—and they worked at night.

Night after night, tirelessly, the goblins descended into hidden caves in the mountains of the Iron Land and collected diamonds, gold, silver, and other precious metals for their neighbors, the elves, receiving nectar and fruit in return.

Goblins were ugly creatures, only half a meter tall, black-skinned with red eyes and pointed ears, capable of striking fear into any human who saw them. Ruled by a tyrannical king, the goblins earned their daily food by toiling night after night and spent their days sleeping.

Their only amusement took place at the dawn of each day when the night twined with the morning. Only then would the goblins sit around a big fire and tell each other stories. Horror stories, of course, because that was all these creatures liked.

And the goblins knew hundreds of stories, each more horrifying than the other, not only from the six enchanted kingdoms, but also from the human world. They had the power to enter the dreams of any mortal, bringing terrible nightmares and bad dreams. They were amused by the fear of evil and lying men, for, I forgot to tell you, goblins only appeared in the dreams of men who did evil deeds, and the powers of these beings could not touch good people.

Amongst all these mischievous goblins lived Art, a goblin so physically similar to his brothers and yet so different from them all.

It was said that when Art was born, two hundred years ago, as the old men told at the fire between the twining of the days, three bright stars of an unusual shape had lined up in the sky, shining brightly in the black night. This happened very rarely, once every few thousand years, and then it seemed, as the old legends said, that someone special was born into the world.

And Art really was special. He was a good goblin, gentle and very peaceful. He did not like to take part in the eternal fierce quarrels between the goblins or to kill the little creatures that lived in the caves: earthworms, moles or other not so nice creatures of nature. He didn't even like haunting the dreams of bad people.

For all these reasons, plus his gentle nature, Art was so different from them that the other goblins had isolated Art, and not understanding him, always picked on him so that he was often the target of other's taunts. The goblins always tormented him by putting dead animals under his pillows or leaving him alone in the most dangerous caves without a lantern or any other source of light. In fact, hey had once locked him in one of the chambers hidden deep in the heart of the earth for several hours.

His brothers were mean, and they always got revenge because Art refused to participate in all their cruel and pointless customs.

But, for as long as he knew, Art lived with a burning desire. He wanted to see the vast forests, the deep lakes, and the enchanted mountains with white peaks without fearing and shielding his eyes from the bright sunlight.

He wanted to go around the whole earth, travel everywhere and make new friends, but this was not possible. No goblin could stand the sunlight, and no goblin had ever left the Iron Land.

It was said that if any subject of the kingdom left these lands, he would never be allowed to visit the land again, and what's more, the evil goblin king would punish him and turn him from a goblin into a gnome, another ugly but powerless creature. Gnomes were on the lowest rung of darkness of all the enchanted beings.

Day after day, life went like this in the land of the goblins: they slept during the day, worked at night, and occasionally spent the mornings at the campfire.

At the end of each week, a goblin would cross the entire Iron Land, carrying in his carriage the things so preciously gathered with hard work from the deep caves in the earth: gold, silver, and diamonds. He was taking them all to their neighbors, the elves.

After long pleas, one fine day the goblins agreed that Art would also carry the precious cargo for the first time.

Art prepared his knapsack with food, got some sturdy clothes and shoes, and led the little horse harnessed to the loaded cart to the Diamond Kingdom.

Located on the borders of the Iron Land and separated from it by a snowy mountain, the Diamond Kingdom was built entirely of precious stones: gold, silver, and diamonds. Old elves with great wings and unprecedented powers guarded its borders, while young elves roamed the entire land.

Elves were good friends with fairies, but also with leprechauns. Along with them, they cast powerful spells and shackled the evil creatures that roamed the land.

After several hours of walking, Art reached the edge of the Diamond Land, left the cart at the golden gate, and then hid in a small pit, waiting.

After an hour or two, three beings of unparalleled, unearthly beauty descended from the sky and stood beside the goblin's cargo of gold and diamonds.

At that moment, Art realized in amazement that he could see them, although it was known from the elders and the old stories told around the fire that goblins could not see high-ranking beings of light. Art could not only see them but hear them. And so, standing there and animated by a sudden courage, he made a decision. He was going to talk to them and ask for their help to escape from the dark and terrible place in which he lived and could never find peace.

If the goblins were beings of darkness and lower rank, the elves were beings of light and higher rank, and that is why their powers far exceeded those of goblins. For this very reason, he knew that the elves were the only ones who could help him escape the tormented life in the Iron Land.

Coming out of his hiding place, with fear and timidity in his soul, Art addressed the oldest of the elves with downcast eyes, "Magnified Master, servant of light, forgive me for my audacity. I know I am a creature of darkness and am not allowed to speak to you, but unlike my other brothers, I can see you in full, not just as air forms, and I can hear you. That is why I humbly dare to ask you for a precious gift."

The elves studied the little goblin very carefully, saw the star that barely illuminated its aura, and realized that they were dealing with a special creature.

Half-light and half-dark, half-good and half-evil, Art was unlike anything they had ever encountered in their travels through the enchanted lands. And the elves had many hundreds of years in which they had roamed the earth.

"What's your story, little goblin?" asked the strongest of the elves.

"I wish, ever since my birth, to see the light, to travel, and to know other lands too. I do not find myself among my goblin brothers. They frighten me and drive me away with their wickedness. It depresses me to work in the dark, and it is very difficult for me to be with others, night after night, in the dark caves. I want with all my heart to be a part of and live in a much better world."

"That's because you're different," answered the old elf. "At your birth, three ancient stars aligned in the sky and gave birth to a new constellation called Aora, and you were gifted with two parts of light and two parts of darkness. Beings born on the night of Aora are said to have special qualities. That is why you do not find your place among your brothers, the dark goblins. This is not common in the Iron Land."

"You see, we can help you, but we want in exchange for these things your immortality," said the second elf. "We urgently need it to give to our king, Almor, who after some battles with powerful forces of darkness, was touched by an evil shadow spell and lost his immortality. You will only live two hundred years on this earth if you give us your immortality, but during this time, you will be able to do whatever you want for a lifetime. You will be able to fulfill all your dreams and travel all over the earth."

Art thought for a few moments, not very long, and made up his mind. Rather than an eternity of darkness and a life in the hidden caves of the Iron Land, it was better to have two hundred years of light, joy, knowledge, and goodness.

He told the elves what his decision was and then they cast a powerful spell. Art immediately fell into a deep sleep. When he woke up, his heart was filled with wonder. He could already see the world with different eyes!

The sun shone brightly, and he could gaze unhindered into the bright rays. He could smell the fragrant flowers and the fresh air, and he could see everything much more clearly. Everything created a state of intense happiness in his little goblin soul, a happiness he had never experienced before.

Cheerfully, he got up from the grass where he had been sleeping and, full of curiosity, started on his way.

Over the course of over a hundred or so years, Art traveled the land far and wide and learned untold stories that add to his wisdom and goodness. He visited all six enchanted kingdoms, roamed the vast plains of the Diamond Kingdom, indulged in long baths in the crystalline springs of the Land Between Waters, and befriended the merry goblins and bright fairies of the Crystal Kingdom.

With only a few decades left to live, he decided to settle in a wonderful forest on the edge of the Crystal Land where he built a small house. All the animals of the forest, all the birds, and even some of the younger beings of light came to the wise old goblin for help and advice. Not even a day passed without Art not doing a good deed: helping an animal in need, taking care of someone sick, or participating in the work in the forest.

But one night, as Art was getting ready for bed, he heard a heartbreaking moan. He took a lantern from his little house and hurried out to see what was happening.

In the middle of the forest there was a great fire, a huge commotion, and in the middle of this fire in an incandescent circle, lay wounded on the ground a little elf.

His wonderful wings were scorched, his skin was burned, and the poor thing could barely breathe. Art looked fearfully at the powerful fire, then at the little elf moaning in pain, and decided on the spot to risk his life to save him. He jumped determinedly into the fire, but blinded by the light of the flames and dazed by the smoke, he fell to the ground.

With the last of his strength, he pulled the elf out of the flames and threw him away from the flame, then lost his breath.

Somewhere in his soul he knew that the end had come, and he did not try to resist. He had serious injuries, severe burns, and everything was going dark around him.

At least I'm not dying in vain, Art thought with the last of his strength. *I saved a life far more precious than my own*. And then he passed out.

Suddenly, he felt surrounded by a cold steam that soothed his wounds and found himself lifted into the sky by an invisible force. In the blink of an eye, Art found himself in the Diamond Kingdom. He no longer felt any pain or burning, and looking around, he saw that he was in the Elf Palace. In front of him in the throne room, lit by a powerful aura, was Almor, the King of the Elves.

"Come closer, little goblin," said the king. "I have wanted to meet you for a long time and to reward you for such noble deeds. You saved my life by giving me your immortality, and now you risked the few years you had left to save my son, the only heir to this kingdom. You are a kind and gentle being, and so to repay you, I will give you immortality again, but also a goblin maiden to stay by your side for eternity. She is just like you, two-parts light and two-parts dark, and with a being like you, you will be happy. You'll never be alone again, even if you won't have the goblin family you were born into anywhere near you. Call Azaleea," the king called and then clapped his hands.

The doors opened and a cute, smiling little creature appeared in front of Art. Her face showed kindness. She smiled at Art in a way that lit up the whole room. Seeing her, Art immediately fell in love and asked her to be his wife.

And so, Art and Azaleea had a big wedding attended by elves, fairies and goblins, as well as other enchanted beings from all six kingdoms.

Then they went off together to their lovely little house in the woods and lived happily for many hundreds of years.

These are the wonderful stories of the Iron Land. Trials, confrontations, fights, love stories, all these happened a long time ago, at the beginning of the world. Kings and queens, princes and princesses, enchanted beings and humans, they all fought so that good would forever defeat evil, so that nothing could destroy and disturb the balance of life on earth.

The Last Patrol

by C. W. Stevenson

Jarris peered into the woods surrounding the farm. A few deer munched on dead grass, the greenery poking through white, half-frozen slush. No other queer shapes moved underneath the shadows of the dead branches.

No sign of an ambush.

Jarris turned his attention away for half a moment to observe the state of his men. The others appeared anxious and had remained so ever since word of the report had come to Round Mountain, one of the Border Protectorate's old hillforts, some several leagues from civilization.

They'd ridden from Tourmaline that morning, questioning folk on their way inland, mostly travelers on the road.

While the old farmer spoke, Jarris's three companions scanned the woods for themselves. Something was amiss. Deep down… they could all feel it, gnawing at their weary minds as they clutched thin cloaks against their freezing bodies. Winter was unrelenting this season.

Jarris didn't want to believe the man. The word of farmers and countryfolk this far into Patraea came with superstition and half-truths. But this many dead? It hardly seemed a quarter-truth, and yet… Jarris felt the cold chill of fear seep down into his bones.

"Aye, they're dead all right. Seen it m'self I did sir."

Jarris nodded at the villager, or farmer, or whomever he was. Just some old soul in ragged clothes, wisps of gray hair atop a wrinkled skull, shivering in the wind. But he wasn't complaining. Jarris was thankful *someone* was talking. Not one man, woman, or child had anything to say as they'd ridden past nearly a dozen homesteads since leaving Tourmaline that morning. Silent as the grave. It was their eyes that spoke. Their eyes would open wide at the mere mention of folk disappearing, shaking their head violently in response before slamming the door. The more polite folk had said something akin to, "We know nothing," and then, they too would slam the door.

Hakkob, half-blind but still one of the finest trackers Jarris knew, spat onto the white ground as he dumped the contents of his pipe to the wind. The two younger recruits Jarris had taken along sat atop their mounts quietly, one plump with a thick, connecting eyebrow, and the other tall and strong, a fifth son of some southern lord. They listened and they watched, as Jarris had instructed. "Listen and learn," he'd told them. "Keep your wits about you."

Jarris turned his attention back to the old man. "How many would you say?"

The old man thought for a moment. "Mmm, I'd say twenty, but then mother never taught me much past that!" And he laughed, allowing a horrid stink of rotten breath to escape the handful of teeth he had left.

Even sitting tall on his horse, Jarris felt the urge to turn his head in disgust, but he was far too polite to insult the only man willing to talk.

"Why do the other nearby farms say nothing?" the plump lad, the one called Ham asked.

Jarris glared at the boy. Apparently, *listen and learn* was easier said than done.

"Silly folk around these parts. Some say they see the Anukai lurking through the woods from time to time. But too cold for their scaly hides if you ask me. Some say other *things*. Heh! But I wouldn't let their words stick in your ears too long if I was you lot."

The chilling wind then blew gusts icy enough to freeze dripping snot. Jarris clutched his cloak tighter to the black chainmail of his hauberk and looked to the woods once more. The grazing deer no longer showed themselves.

Spooked by our rabble. But he wasn't so sure.

Jarris assessed the situation. Twenty dead, possibly more, or maybe less based on the old man's math skills, lying somewhere in the nearby forests. The report of folk missing around the area, some forty kilometers in total, detailed the missing to be predominately hunters, trappers, those who went into the forest to forage, farmers wandering too far from the fields and such. A rabid bear or pack of wolves maybe, but not much chance of that, not in midwinter. More than likely, it was a small group of bandits, starving and desperate. But twenty dead this close together in the thick woodlands of Patraea? That was a massacre, if it indeed be true.

"If you'd like, I can take you there. Like I said, it's not far. Through there." Then, slowly, the old man held up a shaky hand and pointed where the deer had been. The dead branches swayed in the wind as snow blew off their bark. "The blood of the girl that got snatched up went through there. Followed a game trail to the spot I did, sir."

Jarris looked back at Hakkob who stared back, giving no sign of an objection. The tall recruit, Borren, placed his hand on the hilt of his sword, prepared to do battle against the world so it seemed. Ham sat looking at the booger he was pinching between his fingers and then flicked it away.

So, it was settled.

"We'll follow. But if he says stop," Jarris gestured to the tracker, "we stop."

Investigate the missing peasants and report back, Captain Thorne had ordered. As was his sworn duty, Jarris was compelled to inspect the situation further. Perhaps it was the old farmer, the cold, the dark woods looming nearby, or perhaps all three, but Jarris found his courage being tested.

The old man grinned wide, showing the few remaining black teeth that hung from his gums. "It would be my life's honor to assist the Border Protectorate. Garen is my name." With that, he walked in front of them all, leading them to the edge of the woods.

Hooves crunched through soft snow. If there was blood from the missing girl, it had since been caked in the flurries of snow that came and went. At the moment, a fine mist rained down upon them, and somehow that was worse. They hadn't warmed themselves by a fire in two days and counting. For the past two, they'd eaten nothing but cold jerky. Spring couldn't arrive sooner, in Jarris's opinion. The others might agree too. Too many cold nights they and the others at the hillfort had been on patrol or took watch on top of those old walls. Too many.

It would be dark soon enough. Jarris could see the dimming world through the cracks of dense branches. An hour left of sunlight, maybe a little more. Hakkob searched the ground with his good eye as they rode along. When the game trail became too narrow for them to ride, Jarris ordered Borren to stay behind with the horses and wait for their return. Disappointed, the lad said nothing but gave a gentle, "Aye."

"This may yet turn into a hopeless quest. But in case it is not ... I'd have these horses cared for and ready to ride as quickly away from this place as we can." Jarris hoped his words would provide Borren with some understanding, but the lad was young, full of spit and vinegar, his hand always too close to the hilt of his sword. Despite all the boy's strength or skill with arms his noble father had no doubt seen to, what Jarris needed was collectedness, something the passive Ham might contribute.

It wasn't a far walk. The game trail opened to a clearing with few oaks, but still enough to spread one's arms about. The trench was the first thing Jarris noticed. Dug deep into the hard ground, with large lumps of snow spaced out against its edges. The trench ran until it reached the stone. White in color, the stone was massive. If he were standing on Hakkob's giant head, the stone might've *still* been taller. They could all see where two large holes had been carved out of the rock.

Like eyes, Jarris thought, and he could see where blood had trickled down from the sockets, looking as though the stone were weeping red, frozen tears.

Unnerved, Jarris jerked the sword from his side free of its sheath as Hakkob unslung the bow from his back. Ham stood dumb in place, mouth agape, staring at the strange lumps covered in snow beside the trench.

Not only lumps, Jarris realized.

The bodies.

"Gods," Ham whispered.

"What is this?" asked Hakkob, looking around the clearing. Then, kneeling down by the nearest corpse, he examined it more closely, and then another.

"What do you see?" asked Jarris.

"Their throats are slit. All of 'm," Hakkob said. Standing, Hakkob then took an arrow from his quiver and notched it. Turning himself around, he drew back the bowstring and aimed at Garen.

"*You*," Hakkob snarled. "You said nothing of some *fucking* sacrifice. Their blood is frozen down in that trench."

"Heh! And their organs are in the God-Stone! Truly only half-blind. Heh!"

His black teeth and bad breath had been a sign of his heart. Rotten to the core. Jarris held the hilt of his sword tight, his knuckles turning white. He wanted to hurt this man. "Ham!" he called out.

The boy, mouth still gaped at the grisly scene, only turned to see who was yelling.

"Ham, walk back to Borren, tell him to leave the horses and come here. Bring rope."

"I... Back that way?" he whined.

Hakkob kept his bow trained on Garen. "What you afraid of lad? They're all dead, and the only thing this one can harm is your nostrils."

"Heh!" Garen laughed. "I've no quarrel with *them*. I'll be rewarded I will. Always am. I'll have more coin than there be hearts in the God-Stone! Gold!" And the old man bit down on his thumb as if he were testing the validity of a gold coin.

Them. So, someone had put him up to this.

Jarris surveyed the scene as well as the woods behind the clearing. It was silent. But the woods were thick enough for someone to be watching. He wanted to flee. When he'd started his commission as a part of the Border Protectorate, he hadn't imagined there would ever be any *real* danger. Hunt a lone fugitive perhaps. Chase off some outlaws back into the sands of the Barrens. He decided then and there that blood sacrifice is where his loyalty to the Border Protectorate crossed the line. But the recruits and Hakkob were there.

"I am no coward," Jarris said under his breath. His only motivation to stay. Pathetic, and he knew it.

Hakkob didn't hear the silent outburst, but Garen must've.

"Many cowards live, you know? Many cowards ... obey." He used the thumb he'd bit to jam himself on the chest. "Me? A coward, I might be. But I'm a coward who gets rewarded. What'd they get?" Garen looked to the dead. "Nothing now. Heh! Meat for the Tribe!"

Tribe? Only the Hooved Folk regarded themselves as such. But there'd been no valid report of a centaur for years, not in these parts anyhow. If they were, Jarris imagined with wide eyes, then this was a sign they were on the warpath. Folks turning up missing during the day, at night a blood sacrifice, burned farms?

"Hooved Folk," said Hakkob, who'd apparently drawn up the same conclusion. "Gods. We go back. Now, Jarris. There's nothing else to be done here."

Jarris could hardly speak. "But ... the bodies, Hakkob. We must burn them. It'd be proper."

Hakkob walked sideways to Jarris, his gaze and his bow still trained on Garen. "Pox on that. If there's some encampment of *them* out there ... this's got to be reported back."

Jarris shook his head. "These people deserve to at least be burned. After what happened to them, they deserve to be with the gods at the very least."

Hakkob might've objected, but just then, Borren arrived with rope in one hand, his sword in the other. Ham waddled behind him, his own sword drawn, and in the other clutching a map.

"I got a map, in case we get turned around," Ham said, and proudly at that, like he'd solved some riddle.

They all ignored him. Then, Borren grabbed the old man who immediately began to chuckle and babble silently to himself as Borren tied him to a tree. Borren, annoyed by Garen's jabber, tightened the rope enough around his chest to make him fight for air. His chuckling ceased, but his babbling kept going on and on and on.

"Now, burn them," Jarris said, his tone quiet and solemn.

They all piled the corpses into the very trench the victim's life blood had flowed into. Their pale faces bore up at the men of the Border Protectorate. Jarris thought he saw pity in a girl's face. Probably the same girl who'd gone missing last, whose blood they could no longer follow. Her lifeless eyes stared wide into the frozen ground, and her mouth was cracked open, as if to whisper a final thought or prayer. Yet that moment had long passed. And when he found the strength to look again, Jarris decided her look was of pain and terror. A fair mixture of both as her throat had been opened wide. And he knew that if he gazed upon the other faces of the dead that they would tell the same story. Pain and terror. Mostly, it's all there was at the end, and Jarris found himself wishing death in his sleep, old and gray, in his bed next to a warm fire. If only these poor bastards had been so lucky. But then, who is? Who decides one's fate? It was a question for another day though, one for the mystics.

The fire consumed those who'd been sacrificed. The smell of cooking meat was a sickening enticement to Jarris, but it wasn't that which bothered him. No, it was the warmth. He was so cold. They'd all been so cold. The fur mantles around their shoulders, their cloaks, and other garb had become heavy from the snow and light rain that followed. So, Jarris ordered they dry themselves near the embers of the dead as they said prayers to their gods.

Not long after, as the last flame sizzled and all that remained were blackened corpses ready to crumble to ash, Jarris picked himself up from his knees which had dug themselves hard into the now melting slush at the edge of the trench. It wasn't inconceivable to imagine it had been the same position in which all those men and women had perished. On their knees, awaiting to die, waiting for cold steel to open their neck.

"*Achtrachen zen-rauk mierdur.*"

The hushed voice brought with it a darkness Jarris had only been familiar with a few times before. Bringing their attention to the old man, all four of them knew what they'd heard. Garen had spoken the tongue of the Hooved Folk.

"Insolent bastard," cursed Hakkob. "We should slit his throat and be done with it! Burn him next!"

Borren glared knives at the old man. "I'll come to peace with that." Then his sword was back in hand. But before he could take a step further, Jarris chimed in.

"He could harbor information. We take him with us."

Releasing a deep sigh of frustration, Hakkob then replied, "With all due respect, sir, we need to dispose of this evil. He commits himself to death with his own tongue."

"Then we cut it out," Borren suggested.

"No," said Jarris. "He stays alive until our superiors decide his fa…"

The first noise caught them off guard. It was unfamiliar, especially in the woods in near darkness. But as a drum sounded for the second time, it became clearer. Then the drumming was dealt in a constant beat, and it sounded all around them. The blowing horn is what sent them into a frenzy.

"To arms!" cried Borren.

"To the horses!" Ham said as he began running.

"Stay together, damn you!" Jarris called after the lad, but it was far too late. The arrow was already poking through Ham's chest as the second one came whooshing in. It came in like a spear from a bow near Jarris's own height. The second arrow buried itself into Ham's face, crunching through lip and teeth before coming out where his neck met spine. As he fell, the lad brought a plump hand just long enough to feel the hard wood of the arrow. Then he went limp. In his other hand, the useless map unrolled itself from Ham's grasp.

Two of the Hooved Folk came crashing from the game trail, heavy legs pounding against the icy ground. Drums still sounded. Jarris had no idea how many there were as he charged forth.

The largest of the two wielded a spear. Its flat face and giant teeth snarled something in its ancient language. Garen was chuckling insanely now, and he slapped his thighs in celebration. Then the spear came hurling closer.

Jarris fell flat, and he could feel the air pass by his scalp as the spear flew overhead before thudding into a tree. Snow fell from its branches at impact, and the spear vibrated back and forth.

Its huge legs came stampeding forward to crush Jarris's body. The centaur's mangy braids flung around as it came closer, and it spewed white foam from its mouth in an attempt to hurl a final word before the kill.

The arrow caught the creature in its neck; from Hakkob more than likely. Then Jarris dove forward before he could catch a glance at his savior. With a savage grunt, he brought his sword down somewhere on the middle of the centaur's back. It croaked some of its language as it quivered on the ground, but it lay still a moment later, and Jarris had to use both arms to pull his sword from its bloody hide. He almost slipped on intestines as the second creature encroached. Its bow twanged, the enormous arrow zoomed forward, but the loose intestines of the other centaur saved his life as he slipped forward.

Hakkob's second arrow missed as well, and he cursed the names of several gods as he frantically made the effort to pull another arrow from his quiver. Then as he fit the arrow to his bow, the tracker watched as the centaur staggered back. A glint of metal poked through its torso before disappearing, leaving a leaking hole in its wake.

Borren didn't wait for his sword to finish the job, which had suddenly slipped from his hand. So, he pulled the dagger hung through his belt from a sheath wrapped in rabbit's fur and jumped atop the creature's back. They both went tumbling, and the snap of a bone echoed across the clearing. The centaur's own weight had snapped its left hind leg nearly in two, but it didn't have enough time to scream. All that came out was a wet gurgle as Borren's dagger opened the thing's throat. Blood sprayed across the snowy ground.

"They'll skin you alive for that!" Garen yelled. "They'll serve up your balls on a golden platter for tonight's meal! Heh! They…"

Jarris swung his sword at an awkward angle, severing the old man's head from his jawline. Not a perfect swing, but good enough to get the job done. He'd let emotion and duty get ahead of his senses. He should've killed that old bastard the moment he'd confessed. But he was dead now, that's what mattered.

More hooves stamping nearby got his attention, and Jarris ran from the headless corpse, following close behind Borren and Hakkob. He took a last glance at the God-Stone, the terrible, white, weeping rock. At that moment, Jarris vowed to return and topple the thing over. If he lived, he swore he'd do it. He'd come back and wipe out the whole godsforsaken encampment.

The drums continued. If they'd ceased during the fight, Jarris hadn't paid enough attention to realize it. He picked up the pace then despite the burning in his legs; he was at risk of falling behind. Hakkob and Borren were some fifty yards ahead of him. His sweat defied the cold as it ran down his face, and hooves pounded louder as the sound of drums became a distant thing. But he could see the horses now, down the trail, he could see them! So close to their salvation. They'd escape, and revenge would be so sweet.

The other two screamed as they reached the horses. Jarris froze in his tracks and jumped to the side of the trail. He watched through the dense shrubbery as at least six of the Hooved Folk burst from behind their nags. Jarris watched in horror as they tore his men apart without weapons, only brute strength. Two held up Hakkob by an arm each and pulled, removing both limbs from their sockets. Dropping his body to the ground, a stockier creature danced upon his bleeding body, smushing his skull to pulp.

Borren screeched, flashing his dagger around without any rhyme or reason. He was shot full of arrows the next instant, like a hound's muzzle Jarris had seen get too close to a porcupine, the arrows jutting from his body. They shot him still, whooping and yelping a mixture of primal blather Jarris couldn't pretend to comprehend.

The farm.

It was his only chance. There, he could commandeer a horse and ride until it dropped. Of course, he'd do his best to evacuate any unsuspecting villagers, but hadn't that been where Garen had come from? There was no way of telling. But he'd chance it. He'd try for all his guts were worth.

Backing away, Jarris kept low, so much so his knees nearly skidded against the cold, wet ground. His scabbard dragged, making enough racket to make him feel uncomfortable. No noise was good. No noise meant living. No noise meant having arms and legs remain intact. Then as gently as he could, Jarris undid the scabbard, laying it down like a newborn babe. He'd never wanted children before, but Jarris was thankful he still breathed to make that choice.

Continuing his path through the dark, he tripped over logs, branches that punctured his face, and thorns that tore at his hands and the fabric of his cloak when he ran into a bush. He kept going. *Almost there*, he guessed. Though he'd taken the long way around, judging by their trek to the God-Stone he had to be getting close. It was the only positive feeling since seeing his friend be ripped to shreds. Hakkob, a man he'd known for nearly a decade. The end he'd met would be answered with epic retribution, for him, for the lads, and for those massacred. He swore a vow on top of the one he'd previously sworn to the gods.

Lights.

He could see the dim glow of the firelight.

"Gods save me... The farm." He muttered, breathing heavy, even shedding a tear or two. Growing up the son of a merchant, he'd never experienced living in the rat's nests his father had mentioned these farmers call home. In that moment, that light might as well have been the lights of a palace, and the people inside it, royalty. He already wanted to thank them for the hospitality they would offer.

He emerged from the forest. Tattered, beat down from constantly moving, from the cold, from what his eyes had seen. He ran then. Ran through fields where wheat would be planted after this terrible winter. Now he truly was sobbing. For all he was worth, he was ashamed, but for the sake of the gods he was *alive*.

The door to the shack was strong and solid. The owner of this farm was a real carpenter, judging by his fine work. Jarris banged against the door, and again and again, until an elderly woman opened it slow and gently.

"*Horse!*" Jarris managed. He then hit his chest, as if that'd force more air into his lungs. "The Hooved Folk! We must ... must go," he got out, and then he coughed until he spit up phlegm.

"Blasting horse fuckers," the old woman said, her voice shaking with age. "They're a pestering bunch of bastards, aren't they?"

A peasant though she was, Jarris was fairly surprised to hear this woman curse, as old as she appeared.

"Aye," he finally managed. "Please, a horse if you can. My men..." he began, but as soon as he did, the tearing of limbs entered his vision. Swallowing his fear, he continued, "My men were butchered by the Hooved Folk in these accursed woods. I need a horse, citizen. On behalf of the Border Protectorate, I must insist, with most haste if you please."

"You're near to an icicle than human my dear boy. You must sit, warm yourself and then drink something to warm your belly."

Twisting his head back to make sure nothing had followed him, he looked back at the old woman. "No time," he shook his head, "No time. We must make haste."

"Ahhh." She winked at him. "You'll follow me then. Come along." And she nudged past him.

Jarris followed the old woman's slow gait, her bowels passing flatulence with each step. As they walked towards the stables, the old woman asked, "Is my Garen dead?"

Jarris froze.

"Ohhh, that's a *yes* then. Pity. The old bastard had more eyes for their gold than he ever did me. Heh! But then, so did I!" And she laughed, a familiar, almost toothless cackle.

The sound of hooves drew closer, causing Jarris to breathe heavily as he began to panic. Resigned to his fate, he felt no shame as tears began to slide down half-frozen cheeks. He just wanted to keep breathing, if only for a little longer.

They approached slowly from behind the stables, their big eyes glowing white against the firelight from the shack. Moving slowly, almost seductively, their massive shapes came into the light.

Dead in his tracks, Jarris stood there, waiting for what he feared to come.

The Calling Sea

by Sergio 'ente per ente' Palumbo

I t seemed to her that she had been on that shore for a very long time, even though the young woman wouldn't be able to say since when exactly.

Lonely, doubtful, uncertain about what to do, a deep confusion was in her mind, and it had seized her thoughts for a long time, as far as she knew. It was the peculiar state of being bewildered or unclear about something, and certainly there were many things she was presently undecided or forgetful about.

Being short and slender, her face very pale, and wearing a clear, ground-length robe in yellow that perfectly blended with her waist-length chestnut hair, the woman sensed a deep loss of direction. She was unable to place herself correctly in the world by time, personal identity, or location. She only remembered her own name, which was Luighseach, meaning "Torch Bringer," but not much more. A disordered consciousness filled her mind, along with a decided lack of memory and the ongoing inability to recall previous events from her past. All of this came with a great difficulty in trying to focus her attention, and that affected her cognition in the end. Her blue eyes looked around nervously, a bit embarrassed and confused.

Her confused condition was a symptom of something else, something she couldn't figure out.

The inattention she displayed, and her continuous distractibility, led to the deep disorientation that had an undeniable hold on the woman. There was a loss of awareness about her surroundings, environment, and the place itself in which she was. Not knowing what time of day, day of week, month, season or year it really was, the girl simply was unable to decide where to head, or if she had to move elsewhere. So, she stayed in one place under that overcast sky that appeared so far and unreachable from the ground she stood on, just like her mind which was seemingly secluded from the whole world outside.

Only the waves of the endless expanse of gray water that lay ahead of her looked like something alive, while where she stood, and all that surrounded her, resembled a dream world; a fabled site that followed its own rules and ends, whatever they could be. There was nothing next to the young woman apart from that cloth on the sand with some colorful fruits on it. Somebody had probably put those there for her, but it hadn't been for her alone, as she didn't like fruits. This was something Luighseach remembered very well, even though all the rest of her memory looked much darker and more uncertain.

The powerful, ceaseless waves continuously cut into the shoreline. Sloping beaches like that were dynamic landforms altered by the gusts of the wind, the abrasive sand, and the motion of the strong tidal waves that proved to be particularly violent and extensive along those northern coasts. There was an ongoing process of creation and erosion where the longshore current played an important—though almost invisible—role. Of course, the girl didn't know anything at all about the natural process of erosion that altered the shape of that low headland. She only limited herself to admiring and looking at the ground covered in warm, light sand that was interrupted occasionally by widely separated rocks bordering the expanse of water whose ever-changing layers flowed over and then withdrew in unending ebbs and floods. There were a few islets in the open sea, a few birds flying in the air, and some shellfish, but no other human being was there besides herself.

Then Luighseach heard a sound. It was like a voice, but it was in the distance and had difficulty getting to her clearly, as if coming from an invisible wall. Some hidden boundary that separated that shore from its unknown source. If she hadn't known that such a thing was unrealistic, she might think it was something that someone was trying to say, maybe slowly speaking through a bulkhead or a barrier positioned somewhere, but the idea was totally incomprehensible.

Only a few words were capable of reaching her ears and those were meaningless, to say the least. "Here... come... now... here... we... are..."

As those were already unintelligible sentences, her current state of mind didn't provide her with any assistance. Nor did it lead her to find a significant reason for all that. Not that a single thing could be understood. As the waves that hit the coastline and took some sand away, cancelling the features of the ground, the same could be said about the passing of time removing her memory from her and diverting her thoughts towards unexpected directions from where they never returned.

But, as that call resounded in Luighseach's mind, returning to the surface of her thoughts again and again, she began feeling anxious. And worried.

It was just over there in the middle of that sea, where a lost land now submerged beneath the water was said to have once existed. A land where many legends came from. Many ghosts were reputed to live there, and many creatures—who were all that was left of that forgotten country—were continuously busy escaping the misty sandbars in search of comfort and peace, or simply looking for a place to hide. Or for some prey...

She knew very well those Breton legends, the ones that spoke about the fabled John of the Shore. It was said that such calls came from the lost, forgotten souls of those drowned at sea and whose bodies were never recovered. They had long been said to be heard along the shoreline at night crying, "Iou! Iou!"

The girl was also aware of the fact that no person was supposed to send their plaintive call back to those voices in the distance. In her native village—strange that Luighseach was able to remind herself of this particular thing, this important warning—the old people had told her and all the young boys gathered around the fire: "*If you reply once, John of The Shore leaps half the distance separating him from you in a single bound. If you reply a second time, he leaps half of the remaining distance. If you reply a third time, he breaks your neck.*"

It was such a terrible, scary story, Luighseach had always been afraid of it since she was a very young child.

But there was something else. The tone of the voice she was listening to, even though it seemed to be far in the distance, seemed to be one that she was already accustomed to. The girl was incapable of recognizing it completely, but there was a peculiar tonality which didn't appear to be completely unknown. Where had she heard it before?

Just after that voice spoke, a strong wind hit the sand, and the sensation of an incoming storm, a terrible event that was going to reach that place, made her deeply worried. The young woman felt a sort of danger coming up behind her, something evil and very ancient that, until that moment, had kept itself hidden in the forested area at the end of the shore. But that danger was becoming more and more eager, even upset in a way. Hungrier and hungrier, more arrogant and out of control. Luighseach was unable to figure out exactly what could happen. At present, she didn't even know why she was in here and what kind of place this was. But she was afraid of her location, more scared of where she was than of the queer voice coming from the sea, whose tone she thought was milder and certainly more pleasant.

Only when the sense of oppression turned out to be too much for her, having become more and more unbearable, did she happen to notice a sort of shadowed figure. It looked like a black shade, whose offshoots seemed to come out of the trees of the forest in the background, approaching her, longing for her. At that moment, the golden necklace she wore—a classically simple, but very beautiful, ornament that resembled heart-shaped leaves with an adjustable chain—shone immediately, as if a sort of ray coming from the sun or the reflection of the daylight. But since it wasn't sunny out, this fact greatly surprised the girl. The shadowed presence stopped approaching her at once, and a sort of warmth, though strange and only momentary, seemed to cast off the evil and then enveloped Luighseach, briefly illuminating the dim scenery of the shore.

Those few words floated to her ears again. "Here... come... now... here... we... are..." Now the young woman was sure she had to move away from that place, in a hurry. Luighseach still didn't know why, but she knew she had to rush!

"Who are you?" the girl cried out. But there was no reply.

Then suddenly, those words came again to her mind: "If you reply once, John of The Shore leaps half the distance separating him from you in a single bound..." So Luighseach stopped herself abruptly.

But that sensation of a danger at her back made her aware that the evil force was growing again and again and proved to be even more upset at present. Being deeply afraid of it, Luighseach felt oppressed another time, and that sort of inexplicable shadowed figure appeared next to her, looking like something unearthly. Not of her world, for sure. Then, that presence turned into a female-like shape, a tall and thin one wearing a dark robe and with very pale skin adorned with several strange, terrifying symbols. The most striking features were the cruel eyes, surely not human at all, and a prominent forehead. The overall appearance would make anyone feel anxious.

The young woman stood up and ran to the border of the shore, facing the sea, and refused to dream of going back to the place where she had sat previously. She put both of her hands on the necklace, as if she was asking in her mind for the chain's unknown protection, but even that wasn't enough to make her feel better.

"Here... come... now... here... we... are..." The call resounded across the shore for the third time.

"*If you reply a second time, he leaps half of the remaining distance.*" The warning seized Luighseach and made her waver for a while. But the terror of that black shade that was approaching was much deeper now.

"Show ... yourself... we'll help ... you." It wasn't just the words themselves that caused what happened next, but the familiarity with that tone—the sensation that Luighseach knew it—that finally motivated the girl, helping her to make up her mind.

She slowly but decisively put her feet in the water and went into the waves. Luighseach had always been a tomboy since she was very young, and she used to swim in the small lake next to their village, not far from the place where the stone remains of a prehistoric past stood. So, she proceeded onwards, continuing her efforts as she swam, stroke after stroke, desperately.

The young woman swam again and again, moving continuously away from the shore. Departing from the coastline, little by little, until the land in the distance looked like only a thin line she had left behind. But Luighseach didn't stop there. She went on and on. Then, a long wooden shape appeared ahead of her in the open sea, and her confused, strange world changed completely.

The Celtic birlinn rolled among the foaming waves, its single mast displaying a huge light-gray sail while the fair east wind was blowing. Having a high fore and aft along with a shallow, open hull for oarsmen, the wooden ship displayed a rudder in the center. Very different from the steering board seacrafts that the northeastern peoples had on the starboard. Clearly showing a rich heritage of seafaring ancestors—a history that the ship builders had long been accustomed to—there were two men on each oar. So despite being a fairly small vessel, it was capable of transporting up to thirty people. There were also larger galleys used by the Gaelic tribes of Brittany at that time which could hold more than one hundred warriors designed for the purposes of war, but this was not the case here.

Standing upright on the prow, Corfec, the leader of the expedition, stared unceasingly at the gray sea. Wearing a green long-sleeved robe that stopped at the knees, white trousers underneath, and an iron helmet with a central reinforcement and two hinged wings on his blond, long-haired head, the tall young man of twenty-two had his right hand on the short copper scabbard suspended from a chain-link sword belt at his waist. But even though he looked calm and still, the continuous movements his fingers made on the showy hilt clearly revealed his worries and the anxiety he felt inside. As the journey kept going on and on, a sort of apprehension seemed to be impressed on all the crewmembers' faces. They looked busy maneuvering the ropes and the oars, but they didn't dare approach the man in the lead, as if they understood what he was feeling and didn't want to upset him even more. Then suddenly, another seafarer moved forward and reached Corfec. He had a long, chestnut, curly head of hair that blended perfectly with his suntanned skin partly concealed under a large yellow shirt. His muscular hand shook Corfec's shoulders. "You have to get some rest," the man said in a soft tone.

"I can't give in, Sklaer. You know that," the other man replied without moving, his blue eyes locked on the watery expanse that stretched ahead of him. "It was my responsibility. She had been entrusted to me, and I simply had to bring her to the village of our promised allies and then back home. But I failed!"

The other man lowered his head, looking distractedly at his beautifully carved iron bracelet that ran along his right arm. Then he added, "Our chief couldn't have chosen a better man than you for such a duty, I'm sure. Who other than her brother might have been deemed worthy enough to take her to the house of her future husband's father, the leader of the Rhedones? And you did it accordingly, but you weren't able to think…"

"To think that she could suddenly disappear while we were still sailing, without any explanation?" the young man exclaimed. Turning to his friend, he said, "How do you imagine I can go before Guethen, our chief, and tell him that I lost his youngest daughter, my twin sister?"

Sklaer didn't reply but remained pensive for a while. "I don't know, but we have searched this stretch of sea for the whole day, and we have found no traces of her whatsoever. Maybe she fell into the sea, or a wave hit her. Women shouldn't go aboard such a birlinn. It's not your fault, to be sure…"

"It was my responsibility, and mine alone!" Corfec cried out. For a moment, all the other crewmembers stopped their activity and stayed silent. Then all of them slowly went back to their duties. "I endangered our present alliance, too… When one of our women marries, she joins her husband's clan, but she is always going to be a member of our own clan as well. No wife can ever escape that obligation and membership, even though her present husband's clan takes precedence… Now, what am I going to tell the Rhedones? That we, the tribe of the Coriosolites, are unable to remain faithful to our promises of marriage and that we are even incapable of protecting our relatives on board one of our ships along the coast? If this is true, what value have I? What kind of chief could I ever become, Sklaer?"

"You're a good leader" the other stated. "These are dangerous waters, and you have treated our crew and the birlinn well. We haven't stumbled into the bands of insidious plunderers that roam this sea, and no one of us has been injured so far. Probably what happened was due to destiny or because of some…"

"Don't call it sheer chance or the intervention of the damned go…"

"Don't say blasphemous things, Corfec!" Sklaer stopped him. "Don't curse the waves and our travel, please…"

"Our journey is already terrible, my friend. Just look what happened to Luighseach."

"We can't be sure she is dead yet. We must continue our search."

"It's just what I plan to do!"

"All the men are with you, you know."

Corfec turned to the sea again, and grew even more depressed, definitely not taking heart from all that. His friend moved away in order to go back to his activities, when something happened unexpectedly.

At first, it was only a faint impression, a sort of a pink spot against the gray tonality of the waves under the overcast sky, then some yellow shades appeared next to it. It seemed to be a sort of long cloth floating on the water, maybe even a dress ... a woman's dress!

The find had hit Corfec's mind with all of its strength and the man immediately awoke as if from a dream. It looked like her. It must be her! The leader cried out once, twice, then some agitated orders followed, and a great unrest filled the wooden deck as the birlinn changed its course and headed for the human figure that swam across the small waves off the coast. It didn't take long before the ship got to the body that proved to be a girl, and much to everybody's surprise, the features were exactly the ones of the young woman Corfec recognized as his sister.

After she was approached and slowly heaved up aboard, a deep sense of incredulity and stupor appeared on the faces of all the men that crowded the corner where she was lying.

Corfec and Sklaer were the first who reached Luighseach and tried to comfort her given the drenched dress and all the water that covered her slender body. "How are you, my dear?" her brother asked while holding her hands.

The girl was still stunned and had some difficulty figuring out where she was at the moment. A strange worry slipped into Corfec's mind. "You fell overboard, don't you remember?" the man young asked. "We dedicated ourselves to finding you. We have been calling your name continuously for the entire day. Some on the ship said we would only recover your dead body among the waves, but I insisted. I was sure you were alive. We had only to search for you a little longer."

"And you were right, undoubtedly!" Sklaer stated. But the young woman still seemed to be doubtful and seemingly lost, her expression an obvious sign of all that.

"Who are you?" she asked.

"Luighseach! You're Luighseach, my sister." Corfec cried out.

"Me... *Luighseach*?" the girl said, still a bit confused and cold because of the water that drenched her dress.

"We set sail from our native coast to get to the eastern shores. You are the first daughter of Guethen, the undisputed chief of the Coriosolites that rule over the coast which extends west to the far recesses of Brittany. You were promised as a spouse to the son of the chief of the powerful tribe of the Rhedones in order to form a long-lasting, strong alliance with them. Don't you remember? You must have undergone some very difficult moments. I know you suffered much when you were alone. But we did not abandon you, we never lost hope! So, now you're safe, finally you're with us again!"

"I... I think I can remember a little... Maybe..."

"Yes! You are coming to your senses finally! Good Heavens, you're not wounded or exhausted, it's really extraordinary that you got to our *birlinn* in the open sea coming from...."

There were some moments of deep silence, then she completed the phrase of the man "...from the shore. I was just there, or so I think I remember."

"You were on the shoreline? Why? Did you get there by taking a swim? Was it the waves that brought you there?" Corfec had to know, so he kept making inquiries about all that and insisted on knowing what had happened. But the girl still appeared to be a bit uncertain, doubtful, and ill at ease.

Then she replied, slowly and with a dreamy expression on her face. "Yes, I was there alone. There was a thick forest behind me, on the horizon..."

"What forest? There are no forested areas on the coastline around here, as far as we know."

"I don't know, but there was one. Anyway, it didn't even seem as if I was there, but I was almost prisoner of that place. Although, I didn't feel that way. Really, I simply wasn't self-controlled. It seemed like my mind wasn't mine anymore. I was lost... And there was that presence, an unearthly creature menacing to me!"

The other man fell silent for a while, then stated, "We were warned! A powerful, fabled Gerlen, a fairy, lives in the surroundings, and she is a fearful opponent." There was a brief pause and many among the crewmembers exchanged a look. All of them knew that almost every ruin or forest in Brittany had a fairy who was said to live there. They were usually very pretty—but also insidious and unpre-dictable—changelings, so the legends went. Leading a traveler down the wrong path or stealing little valuables were considered harmless pranks by them.

However, some of them were also feared for more life-threatening behaviors. In several legends, a few liked to kidnap humans. "The chief of the Rhedones told us that his elder son was wanted by another person. Truth be told, he was said to be loved by a fairy, a mischievous and dangerous one. They feared that she wouldn't let go of him and allow the boy to marry another wife. He revealed also that the creature would try anything in order to keep that man from having another relationship."

Sklaer whispered, "I was with you before the chief at that time, I remember this, but..."

"But we didn't believe him, of course. Such words seemed incredible and just a fable or lie, so we simply forgot about it. We thought that the Rhedones were just making fun of us. Nothing would stop our alliance, so I acted according to the orders I received from my father. Then you, Luighseach, disappeared during the night during the route back to our village, and we were desperate because we didn't know anything about where you were or the reason why you had gone away. We even thought you might have died, but now I see how things really happened, and it's truly terrible."

There was a long silence on board.

"A common warning is not to eat the fairy food if they kidnap you. It could keep you with the fairies forever." Sklaer added, remembering that old saying and breaking the stillness quickly.

"You didn't eat anything offered by the Gerlen, did you?" Corfec asked, clearly worried.

"No, I didn't. There was some fruit and vegetables on a cloth along the shore, but I didn't eat those as I don't like eating fruit," Luighseach responded.

"Your hatred for those probably saved you. You didn't fall into the fairy's power because of that," Corfec said.

"Why didn't she kill her?" Sklaer asked.

"I think she was unable to do it. Look at her golden necklace." Corfec replied. His friend stared at the classically simple, but wondrously fine, golden design of the ornament that surrounded her pale neck. It resembled some perfect, heart-shaped leaves with an adjustable chain. "It protected her. That object has been in our family for more than fifty years so far."

"Yes, it must be so!" Sklaer responded.

"Why did you get into the sea? Did it force you to swim?" Corfec asked Luighseach.

"I heard a voice calling for me, as if it was coming from the sea. I was afraid of it at first, but I couldn't be at ease in that place. I wanted to move away from the shore. I didn't know why, so I answered that call in the end."

"We've been calling out your name all day long. Maybe you just replied to one of us. Maybe you recognized my voice and awoke from the enchantment of that fairy." Corfec said. As a matter of fact, he had always sensed a special link, some sort of connection with his twin sister.

"We'd better row away from here as soon as possible," another long-haired, middle-aged seafarer said, looking askance at the leader. "I see some very severe rain clouds heading for us. I don't like the looks of those."

"We couldn't weather a storm." Sklaer said, staring at him in return. He was well aware the man was an old salt, so he nodded with a knowing look.

At that time, people thought they might actually run into fairies. It was generally accepted that these dark fairies were something to stay away from in order to be safe. Tangling a sleeping man's hair, stealing little items, or leading a traveler down the wrong path were considered some harmless pranks accomplished by those creatures. In several legends, those mythical beings were even said to like to kidnap humans at times. Which was what had happened to the poor young woman.

Most believed that the fairies lived in an Otherworld. It had been described as being underground, or in hidden hills, or in some ancient burial places, or even across the Western Sea. Nobody really knew where the Otherworld actually was. But maybe Luighseach had been in that secluded, strange place while being kidnapped from their ship.

What an incredible experience it turned out to be in the end, the young brother thought. Having proved to be able to overpower it, to resist such strong flatteries and illusions, along with those evil trickery, she had certainly displayed a far better, more efficacious conviction and presence of mind. Surely more considerable than the men of their crew or the most famous warriors in their village back home, anyway...

Today, Brittany is one of the twenty-seven regions of France, occupying a large area in the northwest of the country between the English Channel to the north and a great bay to the south. The Brythonic culture was part of the Celtic world that once spread over a vast area of Europe and the British Isles, whose tribal territories existed long before Roman rule. But many of its ancient, now-lost legends are still in the air, flowing in the rivers and permeating the terrain itself. At times, if you just dare to listen to their whispers and give ear to the things that the gusts of winds mutter around, you could even notice it. You might perceive the sound that comes from the calling sea, something that an evil fairy attempted to avert with all her tries but finally in vain.

Those words of hope and resistance against the power of evil and the deceptions of the unearthly creatures that always try to divert humans and lead them to the wrong path still fly across that stretch of sea nowadays, like pieces scattered everywhere. Glimpses of a significant, though brief, struggle that took place over the course of the continuous fight between the world of Mankind and the enchanted lands of the mischievous and dangerous beings who kept themselves well hidden in the darkness. Most of the time…

The Wall

By Seaton Kay-Smith

I feel their eyes on me, burning with questions, but the questions are ignorant. They are not questions of what I hope to achieve in finding my target, nor how I came to be where I am now: here, in this dimly lit tavern with its sodden floors and tables of rotted wood, its thick iron doors, colored with rust and locked with three distinct keys, boarded-up windows and gray moss-coated stone walls. Where the incessant odor of festering mildew attaches itself to the air not already claimed by their anticipatory silence.

They are not questions regarding my intentions or allegiances, nor how I, a small-statured woman of nineteen years, managed to survive my journey here with a sword most knights would claim inadequate even for buttering bread.

They are tired questions of small-mindedness and superficiality. Questions I am used to.

They are not concerned by the cascade of demons that have befallen their world, nor the two straight years of rain they have experienced.

They want to know, "Why does half my body bear the scars of fire?"

From my hairline to my hip, the skin on my right side is a deep venetian red. They see the uneven coloring, like moss on a riverside stone, crawling up from my neckline, smooth in texture, wrapping itself around my cheek and forehead.

They had started at my appearance, then after the shock had settled, this congregation of simple townsfolk, gathered in the cold and lit by candlelight with their unwashed clothes and unclean faces, had wanted to know why.

I observe their mouths, slightly open; their eyes, cold, curious and penetrating; the lines made deep between their eyebrows, and

I wonder whether informing them of their shallow ignorance would get me what I want from them.

I have travelled far to get here, traversing drenched pastures made bog by constant rain. I have survived a myriad of horrors along lonely corpse-strewn roads. I feel my goal within sight. It is a fly that has landed in the palm of my hand. It feels as though all I must do is curl my fingers and I will have it. But I know how quickly a fly can move. I must be quick and choose my moment, lest my goals escape my grasp.

To allow my pride to create a vast bridgeless gulf I could have otherwise walked across would punish me more than it would them. I opt instead to humor them.

I pick up a stool, swollen from the damp, place it at the end of that musty table of wet-haired patrons, and begin my tale...

I had been sold to the Bricklayer as a child of two or three. Young enough to have no recollection of my life prior to the arrangement, old enough to receive, in my dreams, flashes of memories depicting my journey there. In truth, I cannot say for certain I was sold. I may have been a gift, or a burden, offloaded to that all-powerful mason.

At seventeen I was as tall as I would be. Fed well and trained. Educated, healthy and obedient. I knew in the days leading up to the anniversary of my birth, that my time was fast approaching. My limbs would stretch no further. I was ready. Unquestioningly, I, along with a few others of my Order, began the slow dutiful march to The Wall.

The Wall was a half-day's walk from our lodgings at the University of the Bricklayer—as it was known to us. "The Hall of the Witch," "The Devil's Lair," or "The Ruins of Hecate" as it is known to those outside of it. We could not live closer to The Wall. The vision of the dead lain neatly on top of each other, naked and raw, vanishing to a point in either direction, is too gruesome a sight for daily observance. We were keenly aware of what horrors awaited us. We did not desire such a constant and grisly reminder of our fate: that cadaverous structure, kilometers across and now a dozen souls high, with its perfectly preserved corpses, bulging in parts, eyes open, limbs stiff. Even over the distance that separated The Wall from the University, it called to us both in sleep and waking.

We did not wish to see it before the time came, nor did we wish to hear the demonic shrieks and the hellish flapping of eldritch wings that echoed through the wet swamplands beyond it. The reason for our grotesque architecture.

On the day in question, we arrived at The Wall in silence and, without hesitation or grief, obediently removed our tunics.

Finding footholds in the divots of our ancestors and kin, we climbed until we reached the peak and lay prostrate in the place we would remain in death for all eternity. In truth, the greatest of my fears came not from the anticipation of the smoldering mortar which would soon be poured upon our naked skin, but from our proximity to the horrible lands The Wall was built to separate us from.

Staring into the sun, I was thankful for its ability to blind, and yet, still I could see in my peripheries the many-legged creatures scurrying about in the noxious fog of the wasteland, their limbs possessed of elbows too numerous to count, each leg springing from a fat swollen body full of faces. The creatures moved swiftly, devouring smaller monsters with each of their mouths, insatiably hungry, acid saliva dripping in feverish anticipation of every meal. I saw, too, even these great beasts fall prey to those who stood above them in that horrible food chain.

The lava-hot mortar could not come soon enough.

Lying atop that rigid stack of sacrifice's past, I stared up at the fault-line in the sky, where day and night met in divine definition; these heavenly tectonic plates rubbing against one another to create deep tremors in the sky. I lay there and listened as the Bricklayer delivered her blessings through tears, paving my friends into that mystical wall of protection. Each of us, her children, the fruit of her life, finally grown ripe enough to pluck.

We had all sworn, late at night, in our simple book-filled dormitories, that we would not scream when it happened. That we would enter the darkness in stoic silence.

Few were able to keep that promise, and as the pained screams drew closer, I knew it would not be long before it would be my turn to be fastened in place by the deadly witchcraft of our all-powerful mother—the Bricklayer. It would soon be my turn to become a glorious brick in that defensive barrier for the good of a kingdom that benefited from our sacrifice, but that did not understand it, nor respect it. It would soon be my turn to scream.

The glare of the sun was blocked by her ceremonial cauldron of mortar, and I saw her above me—red-eyed from crying, mouth dry from *persistent chanting. I steeled my courage and offered the smile I could afford. I was ready. Then, as she dipped her enchanted trowel into the mixture of limestone, crystal, blood, and tears, I heard a sound I did not immediately recognize. It came from the green Eden-like pastures of the kingdom to my right. I had always had an uncanny ability to perceive sound; a gift at times, a curse at others. I did not know which it was at this juncture. Amidst the cracking joints of the demons to my left and the bubbling flesh of my obedient allies, I heard the galloping of horses and the trampling of sunlit grass beneath the heavy hooves of the King's Guard. I heard voices, shouts of horror, gasping. I heard the sounds of stolen breath, of grown men and women sickened by the sight of a thousand dead young-lings stacked upon one another in a wall, kilometers long and ten feet high. I heard tears and retching, frantic voices calling out orders, disquieted equines, and the chaotic shuffling of leather-bound feet.*

Would that I could control this gift, that I could focus on a single sound, but in my stillness and agony, I heard it all.

I heard the unmistakable sound of a bow drawn tight, then the soft airy rush of an arrow as it sailed over my head.

The Bricklayer, despite her over 300 years, appeared ageless. She was omnipotent in many ways. However, even she was confined by certain laws of mortality. The arrow hoped to uphold those laws.

For many years, I thought they had.

I gritted my teeth and swallowed my screams as I felt liquid hit my face and chest. But it was not the scorching mortar I had been anticipating, had been fearing. It was the warm thick blood of my teacher splashing upon my naked body.

I had been saved, as it were, by these men and women on horseback. A wretched, pitiable thing, I was pulled from The Wall by them, and they gave me a cloak to hide my nudity as I was stolen from the place I had spent my youth.

They had forced me to fail at my role as the Kingdom's hidden pro-tector; a dirty necessary secret, thrown into the light and deemed unsa-vory. The King had judged it time to abolish this place of barbarism and "meaningless" cruelty. To bring his kingdom into the light. What a fool he was. For, in this act, it was not the dark, but the light itself that he was unwittingly abolishing. I was dragged screaming—mad, they had said—into the kingdom proper, to begin a life free from slavery and servitude and imminent meaningful death.

Over the years, I heard, in scattered conversations, rumors: the hideous wall, a blight upon our civilized ways, had been torn down. Each ghastly human brick laid to rest below the ground, to rot uselessly below a landscape that, over time would become more hellish, dark and wet, thanks to their removal.

Then I heard another rumor: the Bricklayer still lived.

I soon learned that this all-powerful mystic, with the knowledge and power to banish the dark wet things, had taken a false-name and was living in secret exile as a recluse in the woods that border this hamlet. Gathering what few possessions I had; a sword, a simple bow, a quiver of arrows, and a small napkin filled with food, I left the mold-ridden convent I had made my home and began the journey here...

The horror-stricken faces of my audience slowly morph into confusion. Their issues, small-minded as they were, not with the ethics of the order, nor the implications of my tale, but with my failure to address the one thing which had so forcefully tugged on their curiosity. "But you said the splash you felt was that of the Bricklayer's blood. The mortar never touched you?"

I nod. "The mortar never touched me."

"But..." another begins, their lips quivering. Perhaps they are scared of me, perhaps it is a generalized fear, a common symptom in a world sick with horrors such as ours. It was a miracle they had opened each of the three locks on the tavern's heavy door and allowed me entry to begin with. "...Your scars."

I have scars, it is true, a thin raised line as light as coral, where an arrow from a desperate thief had grazed my neck, a haphazard crisscross of warped flesh on my reddened cheek from being shoved to the ground and held roughly against the uneven gravel of a convent footpath. The nuns hoping to rid my head of its obsession with my past. I had heard their whispers from my room, the low fearful voices of their quorum, fretting that I was permanently tainted by my trauma. Along my back, the memory of whips and planks of wood that wished to beat that trauma out of me.

There is no magic reason for the twists and tangle of my flesh, nor to the coloring this thickened tissue rises from.

I lean ever-so-slightly forward and raise my finger to the right side of my face. Without touching it, I trace a path down past my chin, over my right breast, and to my hip. "This is a birthmark," I tell them, feeling a strange contentment at the anticlimactic nature of my explanation despite my intent to humor them. "I was born this way. It is not fire. It is not magic. It is me." I watch their confusion grow. "I like it, and beyond aesthetics, it is not part of my story. It is simply an overabundance of pigmentation. It is of no concern of yours. A benign vascular malformation." I hear their dry lips part, the heavy swallow of their throats, the soft sigh of held breaths released. "There are bat-winged creatures snatching babies in the night, many-faced monsters stalking the streets, stretched above treetops, hunting for prey. I am not here to talk of beauty standards and physical anomalies to a crowd of damp strangers."

No acid has touched my body, the only acid is that which is on my tongue as I explain my appearance yet again to people who cannot listen like I can, and never even try to.

An uneasy silence follows. Then an older woman with gray teeth, her left arm scarred by the memory of jaws, asks, "Why are you here?"

"I am looking for the Bricklayer."

"Do you wish to finish the job the arrow started?" she asks.

I do not expect for her to understand.

Though it is often cruel, there is a love I feel for this world. A duty. Though they are frequently ignorant, there is a tenderness I feel for the people. I have a yearning to feel sunlight on my naked body once more. To see the blue of the sky, to walk in dirt, not mud. To be dry and safe. To not hear the flapping of those wings, the hellish shrieks in the night. To walk as human, not merely as prey.

We had been plied with books at the university, kindling to light the fire of our understanding. We had our eyes opened to the beauty of the world, the fragility of it. From the weeds to the people, the soft dirt of the paths to the hard stone of the houses. The harmony of it, the improbability. There is shadow and there is light, and while light can *create* shadow, the shadows born without light are even darker.

The people are suffering. So too are the trees and the beasts that once found shade beneath them. The lives The Wall had protected far outnumbered the lives that had been sewn into it. For the magic to work, each brick must be willing. We were told nightly of our freedom, our ability to walk away. Our choice. We were educated, not only in the arcane, but in consent and self-worth. We were taught to think critically, to think for ourselves. We were presented with the facts and instructed to decide our *own* fates. We were loved. We were mourned. We were useful.

"Do you wish to kill her?" the old woman asks, repeating her question.

I hear the question echo in the silence of that mildew infested tavern. I feel it in the judgmental eyes of its inhabitants, their eyebrows knitted together. It bounces between them, hanging heavy in the damp air.

"No," I say, shaking my head. "I wish to reinstate her."

The Azure Knight and The Swamp of Sleep

By Cathy Kirk

The Azure Knight was described by different names: saint, immortal legend. Regarded by some to be a thousand years old and theorized by others to be a benevolent spirit. As such, there are many tales of their bravery, like *The Lake of a Thousand Tears* where they rescued a prince trapped between the siren-made waves. That is not the one that shall be recounted.

Below follows the knight's last adventure: *The Azure Knight and The Swamp of Sleep.* The beginning of the story always varies. Some say a witch read the palm of their hand in a rare moment of ungloved vulnerability and read their destiny. Others claim a monarch from a faraway forgotten land requested their assistance. There are even others that say the knight was driven by the very human desire to disappear for a while. I begin the tale thus:

The Azure Knight went to the forest to get lost. Accompanied by the silver dagger with their family name inscribed in its handle and the blue helmet that always covered their face, they stepped into the tree line. Many have wondered why they wanted to get lost. After all, the Knight was, still is, a legend, a God amongst believers, the hero of the people... Could it have been heartache? A quest from some capricious entity which is felt yet never seen?

The leaves fell, as if crying for them. The wind seemed to whisper "Go baaack... Return from hence you cameeee..." while enveloping the Knight like the cold arms of their mother, attempting to push her out. The Azure Knight paid no heed to the pleas, enduring the terrible winds that tried, in vain, to blow her back to a home they were no longer familiar with. The finale shall remain the same. The eyes

remain fixed on the road in front of them, determined to reach their destiny: the Swamp of Sleep.

LOCATION: RUJABU'S VALLEY

Wet earth, trees, and the wind turned into rocks and heavy silence, the blue armor the only color in the dreadful landscape. The gravel moved under the sabatons, the sound echoing through the barren land. The empty terrain morphed into a rocky mountain in a blink of an eye. It was as if it had materialized in that exact moment. The weary knight approaches, inspecting the supernatural formation, reaching the conclusion that, though it resembled a mountain, what had appeared in front of their eyes was more akin to a steep ramp with a winding gravel trail that reached its peak.

Determined to continue the journey and not seeing any way around the gargantuan structure, the Knight resolved to climb the "mountain." The further they walked, the steeper the path got, eventually becoming a wall which the knight climbed, discarding everything from the heavy suit of armor except for the helm, leaving them clad in a blue shirt and blue riding pants. The rocky protuberances sliced their palms, leaving behind a path in blood and skin like Gretel. Only instead of Hansel, the blue speck in the gray sky had the distant and disinterested voice of their father for company.

Before you pull yourself up, be sure your grasp is firm. If it's shaking, stop and rest. Now inch yourself up. No, no I cannot help you. You must learn to do it by yourself. That's it, keep going. Ignore the pain, the skin will grow back.

The top of the ramp was within their reach, and for a moment, the Knight was once more a child, looking up at the outstretched, calloused hand of their father, but in a blink of an eye, it was gone. With much effort, they heaved themselves up to solid ground. Laying on their back, they assessed the damage done to their palms.

"Nothing to worry about," they murmur.

The figure in blue sits down in front of a cave to rest. They stretch their exhausted legs and look up at the sky, eyes widening when they find a sky full of stars when moments ago it was a dull gray. They search for a familiar constellation, however the sky that they so tenderly looked at often was now a stranger. The stars start to spin like dandelion seeds, a face emerging from the strange cosmic dance; a face with exposed bone and muscle, revealing teeth usually hidden by a cheek. The right eye was milky while the left one was barren. Although disfigured, the face was kind, putting the usually distrustful knight at ease. The voice, warm and smooth like summer wind, seemed to be coming from right beside them.

< What you run from will help you. >

The floor begins to shake, an enormous shadow projecting on the cave's wall. The Knight stands, left hand resting on the concealed dagger, rising in front of a chest made of rock.

The creature's bald head grazed the top of the cave. It had sheep's eyes, a bulbous nose, and feet the size of the Knight.

A troll, thought the knight, keeping a neutral expression.

When planning for their journey, the Azure Knight had naturally assumed they'd see landscapes and monsters that did not belong to the natural world. However, a troll had never crossed their mind for they had never seen one in the flesh, only in pictures in the dusty tomes of their family's library.

"The sun turns the troll into stone," their father had told them one day with a monotonous tone, as if already tired of the conversation he had initiated, wrinkly hands grasping an axe. "That's why if you see a rock formation that looks like it has a big nose, it was once a troll."

So, this one is already dead. A tangible ghost.

Slowly, they draw the hidden weapon. The creature's eyes follow the movement.

"Human, do you think that will hurt me? Look at my skin, what knife could kill me?" questions the troll.

The Knight considers the creature's words. They raise their empty hands.

"Who are you that roams my valley?" Rocks fall from the cave, answering to its voice.

"You may address me as Sol," the Knight responds.

The creature notes the phrasing of their response. "I am no fairy. Your name serves me no purpose."

"I promised someone I wouldn't tell anyone. Promises are serious things. What do I call you?"

"Rujabu"

Their instinct told them that the name the troll gave them was its real name.

"Why are you here, Sol?" The emphasis on the fake name would sound like scorn if its voice wasn't so neutral.

"I'm just passing through this valley; my destiny does not lie here. I did not know the valley belonged to you. I apologize and humbly request you let me continue my journey."

"What is your final destination?"

"The Swamp of Sleep."

Its face betrayed no reaction. "You must give me something that solely belongs to you if you wish to continue your travels through my realm."

The troll approaches the Knight, laying an enormous hand upon their head.

"Like your hair."

Sol shook their head. "The hair isn't mine."

Rujabu blinked. "Is it not upon your head?"

"Yes."

"Then it can only be yours."

The Azure Knight shook their head. "This hair does not belong to me."

"Then to whom does it belong to?"

"It belongs to my mother. It is her that cuts and braids it. She does what she wants to it, disregarding my opinions. Hence, the hair is not solely mine."

The giant considered their words. "And the eyes?"

"These I inherited from my grandmother. They belong to the places I have seen and all the people I have loved. They are not mine alone."

The troll mulled over the answer. It stretches its arm to touch the place where a womb may be, but before he could make contact, its wrist is firmly grasped. Its skin is as cold and rough as the Knight expected.

"Nothing in this body belongs solely to me, least of all what you think is there."

The stone creature frowns. "Then tell me what you can give."

The Knight didn't hesitate. They removed the boots that protected their feet from the hostile ground and presented them to the giant.

"It was I that built these shoes. The leather belonged to me, as well as the tools of the trade. These shoes are the only thing that are solely mine."

Rujabu pondered the human's words. They did not stutter or tremble before him like other travelers. The posture of the young person was of someone who, simply put, did not care what might happen to them.

The stone ghost accepted the boots, disappearing inside the cave without another word. What more was there to say?

The Azure Knight looked at the sky. The disfigured face was gone, but they could still feel their presence. They looked back. The cave and its inhabitant were gone.

A tangible ghost.

They continued their journey.

LOCATION: THE BRIDGE IN THE FOREST OF SORROWS

With torn socks and bleeding feet, the Azure Knight arrives at her next destination: The Forest of Sorrows. The sunrise makes the morning dew sparkle like crystals on a chandelier. The grass caresses the sore soles of her feet, urging the Knight to stop and sigh. Their ears eagerly await the twittering of birds or the sound of tiny paws scurrying through the lush garden, yet silence permeates the forest.

"When you hunt alone, remember this: if you do not hear the singing of birds or branches breaking, you are in a predator's territory." *Their bloody hands prevented them from hiding their face from their mother's fiery eyes, her face covered with the same carnage as their hands. The viscera on the two people were nothing compared to the state of the deer behind their mother.*

The Knight hides behind some foliage. Their heart is beating so fast they can't help but imagine it was stretching the skin on their chest. They grit their teeth.

Inhale one, two, three. Exhale one, two, three.

The thought twirls, jumps and drags through their mind, the same one so often prayed behind a bow and arrow and recited once more when flesh was separated from bone, always under the watchful eye of their mother.

I must not panic. If I do, whatever is hiding here will kill me.

Little by little, they calm down. The Azure Knight remains crouched, the grip on the dagger so firm their last name is tattooed on their injured hand. The open wounds on their palms sting, their eye twitching the only tic that shows they are in pain.

The sun rose, shined, and painted the sky lilac. The morning dew gave way to unbearable heat, the sweat drips on her eyes, the muscles scream in pain; the Knight remains a statue. Their gaze slowly sweeps over the silent clearing.

Whatever hunts these woods cannot be a normal animal. Even a wolf would not be able to quiet the birds or squirrels like this. Whatever it is, I doubt I can negotiate with it like I did with the troll...

They were speculating this when night falls, and an innocuous sound freezes their blood: the ruffling of bushes. They look left with narrowed eyes, body tensing. A scream of pain makes their hands shake, but the Knight remains in their hideout, the taste of copper fills her tongue with the effort to not act. Another scream echoes through the forest before the creature comes out of its hiding place. A tall woman emerges from the foliage, dressed in funeral attire with teary eyes, sharp nails, and vulture wings. The Knight's heart jumps to their throat.

A banshee.

"Banshees announce when death is near," their mother tells them while combing their hair. "Although they are not responsible for said death. If you ever encounter one, run."

Slowly, eyes never straying from the creature, they move toward the edge of the bush, stopping when the monster switches position. The wings seem more agitated. The Knight must get away from it as soon as possible but also knows one wrong move spells their death.

The banshee's head contorts with a *crack*, black eyes fixing on the Knight's hiding place, nostrils flaring. For a few moments, neither move. The heavy silence returns. Sweat pours down the prey's face, the predator's eyes following its trail until it drips onto the forest floor. The monster attacks with a deafening screech.

The creature slams into the Knight. The two bodies soar through the air, the grass that not long ago offered some relief now stabbing into the human's back. The banshee continues screaming while tears run down her face, eyes full of anger and sorrow. Blood drips from the dazed knight's ears. The monster raises her paw above her face, claws reflecting in the moonlight, exposing her flank and handing the Knight the opportunity to stab it. The unexpected act makes the banshee retreat. The prey gets up and away from the predator. They now stand face to face, covered in each other's blood, waiting for the other to attack first. The monster smells its own blood, wings raising to appear even larger; the Azure Knight mimics the pose with their arms, backing away slowly. Once they reach the edge of the clearing, they turn and run, an animalistic yell signaling that the beast is after them.

The trees switch positions, affording the Knight only mere seconds to avoid colliding into them. The tree bark scratches against their body, the Azure Knight cursing themselves for leaving a trail of blue fabric. Their lungs burn, but they couldn't stop. They could feel the beast's breath on the back of their neck. They dodge a branch, hearing the monster fall for their own trap. Taking advantage of the creature's carelessness, they Knight firmly plants their right foot on the earth, and using the momentum from their body's rotation, buries the dagger in the beast's stomach. The Knight is showered in the monster's scorching black blood, screaming in tandem with the animal, the blue helmet reflecting in the creature's bottomless eyes.

The beast retreats to the foliage again. The knight does not waste time celebrating, resuming their desperate run, even though the forest returned to its uncomfortable silence, broken only by their heaving breaths. The human does not know where they are going, blindly guided by adrenaline and instinct.

They spot an opening curtained by rain, and laughs, relief giving them a burst of energy. They are so close they can smell the wet earth and hear the gentle rain drops ricocheting off the puddles. They stretch their hand; the tips of their fingers graze the water.

A body clashes against theirs.

"NO!"

The Knight strikes blindly, sometimes hitting their target, most of the time tearing through empty space. Clothes and skin tear, they kick the creature in its stomach and crawls toward the bridge between the two worlds. Their ankles are grasped, and they are dragged backward, a trail of broken nails and blood carved into the ground. The prey kicks and grabs at anything they can reach, but all their efforts are for naught. The predator drags them to a small clearing of its own making, trees enclosing both in, the skylight the only exit.

"LET GO OF ME, BEAST! LET ME OUT!" screams the Knight, anger taking over their mind.

The creature is hit by the bitter words. Her coal eyes fill with pain, as if it were capable of understanding the words spoken by its prisoner or, at least, the intent behind them. This only fueled the fire burning inside the knight, making them kick the air, keeping the creature away from them.

"You do not have any right to be upset!" the Knight continues. Their voice trembles while their tongue spits unforgiving poison. "You attack me, then have the gall to whine because I defended myself? That sad face makes me sick to my stomach!"

Fury took over the monster, screaming in response to the Knight's words.

Days and weeks pass until they couldn't tell one apart from the other. The beast would bring the prisoner food, which initially they refuse to consume. However, hunger and thirst broke their spirit. The guard and the prisoner remain in opposite sides of the wooden cage. The monster would try to approach the prey and the prey would try to escape, both unsuccessful in their attempts, both covered in wounds inflicted by the other. The Azure Knight looks longingly at the falling rain, so close they could still smell petrichor.

One day, while they dreamed, the Knight turned beast was visited by the kind man. With a sweet and gentle smile, he asked:

"Have you so quickly forgotten, Sol?"

"That is not my name." Their own voice frightened them. Did it always sound like that? They can't recall.

"It is the only one I know... Unless you wish to tell me your real one?"

Sol pressed their lips together and shook their head. The man's smile widened, remaining kind.

"Ah, so you have not forgotten your journey and all you have yet to do."

The Azure Knight swallows their tears. "I cannot escape. I have failed."

The man extends a greenish hand, the Knight automatically backing away. He stops, and the figure in blue looks down in shame.

"I apologize," they whispered, tears hidden behind their helmet.

"I should be the one apologizing. I forgot life has not been kind to you. I simply desire to look at your hands."

"My... my hands?"

"Last time, I did not have a chance to do so. Do they still hurt? Or does anywhere else?"

The Knight falls on their knees, hand clutching their heart. The smile and kind words that they feel they do not deserve were a devastating blow. The man sits next to them, careful not to touch. He whispers a song in a long-forgotten language that puts the Knight's soul at peace. When the tears stop and their breathing goes back to normal, the man continues speaking.

"The world was also unkind to the woman who torments you."

"That is not an excuse to hurt me."

"It is not. Even still, try to offer her the kindness you were not given."

"She does not deserve it."

"She does not. Give it to her all the same."

When they wake up, the Knight knows what to do. They eat with pleasure. They let the banshee approach them. They sit side-by-side in silence. Since it wasn't attacked, the creature rests her head on the Knight's shoulder that in turn runs their fingers through her hair and murmurs songs that their mother sang to them.

Days passed in this performative peace. The creature lets the Knight guide her to lie on her lap. She is so relaxed she does not notice when the Knight pulls the dagger from its hidden place. Her eyes open when she feels ruthless silver upon her neck, but it is too late. Her throat is slit with cold efficiency. She does not feel the warm tears that fall on her cheeks; however, she feels the trees that guard them age and turn to dust. The Azure Knight pushes the creature off their lap, heart racing but with an even breath. She delivers a final blow to the skull, creating a macabre Excalibur. The Knight looks down at the hands that committed such treachery; scarred, crooked, calloused hands. Ugly hands to reflect all the atrocities they have committed in their life.

"They were never clean to begin with," they tell no one.

They exit the cage turned tomb, limping toward the portal, the wounds and fatigue slowing them. In the forest, the singing of birds at long last could be heard. They lock eyes with a trickster fox. The Knight waves at them.

With a sigh, they go through the portal.

LOCATION: THE SWAMP OF SLEEP

The rain is a warm blanket. Their battered feet are softly cleansed and treated by the rushing water. Sighing in relief, the Knight carries on their way. Sometimes they step on the roots of countless *Nyssa biflora* that guide their way. While the trees in the forest are an oppressive presence, the ones in the swamp radiate a soothing energy, the drops that fall from their leaves softly stroking their covered face.

The music from their dream echoes through the setting, increasing in volume the closer the Knight gets to its source: the end of their journey. Outlined against the watercolor sky sits a man with long brown hair intertwined with flowers and moss under a willow tree. The man raises his head, revealing hazel eyes, and though the face is not the same, the Knight knows it's the same man that always helps them, evident by his soft voice and the kind smile directed at them.

"Welcome, Sol. You made it."

The Knight trembles before the benevolent being, guilt and shame once more taking ahold of them.

"She would never let me go. She..." The Knight swallows around the lump in their throat, looking away. "I did not have... I do not deserve..."

It was like a hand was strangling them, the words dying between their teeth. Their hands start to shake, their family name drenched in blood that would never dry. They would never be clean.

"Sol," the voice cuts through the invasive thoughts, "your quest is over. Remove the helmet and sit by my side."

The Azure Knight hesitates for a few moments, but the man's gaze was comforting. They could not refuse such a simple request. They remove the helmet, and there, the great Azure Knight stood. The hero of the people. The legend rumored to be a thousand years old. There they stood, bare, with blood running from lips to chin, dark brown eyes underlined by dark eye bags, sweat-matted black hair, and crooked fingers, broken and mended and broken again. The legend, the revered: a young body covered in new and old scars never fully healed. They lower their gaze and sit next to the man, knees touching. The azure helmet that defined them now buried in the mud.

"Why did you take this journey?" the man inquires.

"Where I come from, they tell stories of this place. Of you. The details of the quest are not clear, and the ending is never the same, nor the beginning. Though the entrance remains consistent: a peninsula like forest in a lake inside another forest. The cold wind pushes until you reach the other side, another dimension maybe. Are you a hero or a villain?"

"It is a matter of perspective. To your loved ones, I'll be a villain."

"I doubt I have any left."

A comfortable silence settles between them, the former knight lost in their thoughts, and the man peacefully waiting.

"I made this journey because I'm tired," they whispered, defeated. "The weight of the crown forcibly placed upon my brow, the duty I never asked for..."

The wounds on their face resemble wrinkles on a time-weathered face, dark eyes like opaque glass.

"I understand."

A bit of leftover anger bubbles to the surface.

"Do you? Do you understand what it is like not to have known a kind touch? To crave it all the same, yet recoil in fear when offered it? Do you understand what it is like to be put on a pedestal made of sand, to be gazed upon like a distant God or some entity that none are brave enough to approach unless to ask for something? I was not blessed with strength like Hercules or cunning like Odysseus, these were traits I was forced to adopt lest I invoke the anger of my makers, the parents and followers alike... Because love. Love is not something deserved; it was earned through blood and pain, mine or others. Not unconditional, but fickle. And Heaven's help me if someone saw me stumbling."

The man is unfazed by the outburst. Instead of reprimanding the person next to him, he holds the self-proclaimed monstrous hands between his own, rubbing soothing circles with his thumb, dropping kisses on them.

A blessing.

"I'm so tired," they repeat, shoulders drooping.

"Rest your head on my shoulder and rest, child. Rest for as long as you need."

"What if..." they pause and swallow, "What if I need forever?"

"Then forever you shall stay. I love your company, quiet or talking."

So, they do. The man is warm, and his voice is a lullaby.

"Are you going to tell me your name?"

"...Sol."

"Tell me how you got here, Sol."

"The Azure Knight was described by different names: saint, immortal legend, regarded by some to be a thousand years old and theorized by others to be a benevolent spirit; as such, there are many tales of their bravery, like *the Lake of a Thousand Tears* where they rescued a prince trapped between the siren-made waves. That is not the one that shall be recounted..."

Beyond the Shadows

Patrícia Sá

A name. The way to address someone or something. It describes more than identifies. If it identifies, it is but a shadow. What we at the Hailbrand University aim to achieve is to find a path to reveal the true forms of our world of shadows. The True Names. The very essence of things.

At Hailbrand University, we do not believe in false names. How are you to learn of the world's true essence if you hide yours?

Here, you must go by your True Name. But the Fäe rule still applies: you are never to give it to another creature.

The books were heavy in Mona's arms, yet no matter how many she brought with her, she felt like it would never be enough. She was doomed to be a failure, never to reach her true potential, if such a thing even existed. Miss Dahlia seemed to think so, at least.

"You are quite close, Mona," she'd said that afternoon after class. "Go over the materials again. If the issue persists, come see me."

As if she hadn't done this same thing every day for the past couple of months.

She couldn't figure out what was wrong. No matter how many times she practiced her magic, everything remained cloudy. She could only see silhouettes in a never-ending mist, shapes with no real distinctive qualities. Her classmates had shouted their assignments' True Names already. Hers was the only one still unnamed. What was worse was that this was a collective task; no one was to move on to the next assignment without every True Name revealed.

She felt a bump and lost the precarious balance she'd achieved. A mountain fell, heavy stones landing on her toes. Her shout echoed in the library, and several heads turned toward her. The studious silence grew heavier.

Mona turned, finding her classmates Troy, Felicia, and Gregory, looking at her with wicked grins.

"You should watch where you're going, Mona," Troy said. "A weak thing like you doesn't know enough Names to catch yourself."

"Yes, are you even a faery? Certainly not a proper one," Felicia added.

"Maybe she's a shapeshifting gnome," Gregory said, and all three of them broke into loud peals of laughter. Mona's fists clenched.

"Very clever," she said. "You talk to your Queen with that mouth?"

"Don't get smart with us," Felicia said. "It's because of *you* that we're so behind on assignments. You're lucky no one's hexed you yet."

"I'd fix whatever it is you're doing wrong fast," Troy said. "It would be a shame if you had to leave the university. Your mother would be *so* disappointed."

"How about you mind your own business?" Mona said and turned to walk away, tired of listening to the same nonsense. She knew her mother was the reason why anyone still deemed her worthy of attending Hailbrand University. After all, having a daughter of the greatest Priestess of the Fäe as a pupil was one of the highest honors a magic school could hope for.

However, Mona was proving to be the complete opposite of her mother. Her peers openly showed their disdain; her professors felt only exasperation when they didn't outright despise her. Take Miss Lucilla, who always seemed ready to dump her headfirst into the Storm Caldron. Or Mr. Bright, who barely even spared her a glance anymore.

Mona was really starting to think of giving up.

"*You will be one of our kind's greatest,*" her mother's words would ring as soon as the thought crossed her mind. "*I see it. You'll tap into a Name never before discovered, and you will change the world.*"

Will I, truly? Mona questioned herself.

That day, she'd stayed later than everyone in the library. She went through most of the books she'd picked out; her eyes were red and tearing up, and the paper cuts on her hands went unacknowledged. Every once in a while, she would look into the True Realm, and the fog was as dense as usual. She tried walking toward the silhouettes—black forms that looked no different from one another. Mona wanted to scream. What was she doing wrong?

She decided to flip through the final book's pages but frowned upon seeing the cover. She didn't remember bringing this one. It felt fragile, with yellow-brown pages and a moth-eaten dark-green cover. The title was inscribed in a language she couldn't read; the Old Tongue, if the twirly characters were anything to go by. Out of curiosity, she flipped through the pages and was surprised to find that it was written in Novel Tongue. They were a mix of incantations and recipes for potions, most of which she'd never read before.

Mona reached a page with a shadowy form illustrated on it. There was only a white smile on its face. The bold letters read, *Little Helper.* Intrigued, she skimmed through the text. It appeared to be a spell to summon some sort of entity to help with tasks. Perhaps a brownie? Or a gnome? A sylph? One sentence caught her attention:

There are no limits for the Little Helper. He will follow his master's orders and fulfill their every wish.

Mona worried her lower lip between her teeth. These sorts of spells reeked of forbidden magic. But this "Little Helper" sounded perfect. Perhaps she'd be able to ask it to make her magic better so that she could finally learn something's True Name and not be a burden on her peers and professors anymore. Bees buzzed guiltily in her stomach. She was supposed to unlock her magic by herself. But what else could she do? She'd tried everything, and everyone's expectations were rocks on her frail shoulders.

She voiced the spell.

Mona was lying in bed, still awake. She couldn't understand what she'd done wrong this time. No "Little Helper" appeared. She'd read the spell again and again, louder each time, so much so that Miss

Evadina kicked her out of the library. "I can't have you bothering the Tomes!" she'd said. Mona had gone straight to her room, feet dragging over the marble floors. She thought of packing her things in the morning. It was hopeless. She had no magic in her. She'd never heard of a magic-less faery. Perhaps that was what her mother had meant, when she said she'd be unique among their kind.

The moon chimed with every passing hour. Sleep evaded her still. She'd tried to stifle her cries as much as she could; the walls weren't thick enough for the sound to go unheard. She'd long lost count of the moon rings. The night felt endless.

"Is Master going to keep crying like that?"

The voice was high pitched like a squeak. Mona jumped out of the covers, and her eyes went wide as what looked to be a four-winged rabbit stared at her with large lilac eyes.

Mona screamed.

"Argh! Please do not make those loud noises, Master, my ears are sensitive!" the creature said, its fluffy black ears lowering.

"W... What are you?" Mona said, grabbing her wand and pointing it at the creature.

"That will not be effective, Master. You'll find I'm immune to most Fäe contraptions," it said before bowing. "You summoned me, Master. I am your Little Helper."

"My... my Little Helper?" Mona blinked and a smile bloomed on her face, "So it worked? I can't believe it. It worked!"

"Yes, quite," the Little Helper said. "You can call me Jack."

"Oh, my stars, this never happened! This is the first successful spell I've cast. What should I do?"

"Well, you can start by telling me what my orders are."

"Your orders?" she asked. "Oh, yes, that's what you do. What are you exactly?"

"I'm a Little Helper," Jack said. "I'm here to do your bidding."

"So, I can ask you anything?"

"Anything!"

"Anything at all?"

"Yes!" Jack winked. "There aren't many things I can't do."

"All right." Mona rubbed her hands together and tried to quell the burning flames licking her chest. "I want you to help me reach my full magical potential."

"Oh, exciting!" the Little Helper jumped on the bed. "A powerful Priestess in the making, are you?"

"What?" A stone fell in her stomach.

"Don't be surprised, Master, I can see it." Jack laughed and it sounded like bells. "I can also see your Name, but I need you to give it to me so I can help you."

Dread and a prickling of regret buzzed in Mona's head. The soft glint in its eye and the sharp smile like the one in the picture made her think that maybe it wasn't as innocuous a creature as it looked. What had she summoned?

"I sense your hesitation," Jack said. "Understandable. It is, after all, your most prized possession. But let me ask you this: what would you rather happen? Keep on failing every task, until you're eventually cast out of the Fäe, doomed to live in the Wilderness with the sprites, and the hobgoblins, and the ogres?" Jack extended a paw. "Or would you rather make a deal and be the faery your mother wants you to be?"

The mention of her mother left Mona conflicted. Ever since the first days in her cocoon, she'd felt her mother's wish for her to follow her footsteps and become the next great Priestess once her mother's powers wilted and she had to Move On. Mona's fate was branded to her heart, and every day, she felt the burns of it aching. If she failed, how could she face her mother? What would she do if she was to be a magic-less faery? Would she be thrown in the Bottomless Well where dragons and great serpents were said to dwell? Would she be sacrificed to the stars? Sent to a human village to be hunted?

There really was no choice.

"I will give you my name," Mona said. Jack's grin widened, teeth sharp as fangs.

"Perfect! Your wish is my command.

Jack hadn't left Mona's side since they'd made their agreement. He'd said that was part of it, that Mona was absorbing his essence so her wish could be fulfilled.

"Is that not dangerous to you?" she'd asked.

"On the contrary," Jack said. "Your name gives me all the sustenance I need."

Despite her reservations, she couldn't deny that Jack's power was having an effect. The mist that always surrounded the True Realm grew clearer, and soon she was able to read her first True Names. Her classmates and professors had been speechless. How could a hopeless pupil suddenly show such progress? Many of her peers began asking Mona for advice on their studies. Some even looked up to her, the living proof that no matter how long it took, they would triumph in the end. Others, however, weren't as taken by her improvement.

"How did you do it, freak?" Felicia said one day. Jack was giggling in Mona's bag, and she hoped it went unheard.

"How did I do what?"

"Don't play dumb!" Felicia screamed. Mona could feel the heat of her rage from where she stood. "How did you get so powerful? Two weeks ago, you couldn't lift a feather to save your life! Did you make a deal with a sylph or something? Are you even Mona? Did she hire a shapeshifter?"

Felicia was getting ever angrier, fingers alight in orange flames. She was the daughter of a King and a very skilled faery, one of the best in their class. Despite her fast growth, Mona wasn't sure if she could take her in a fight just yet.

"Calm down, Felicia," she said, raising her hands in a placating gesture. "There's no need for a fight."

"Calm down?" Felicia shouted. "I've worked my wings off to get where I am! I had to learn how to see into the True Realm when I could only cast a few sparks. My father, my entire kingdom is relying on my magical proficiency. What do you think will happen when they learn I was bested by the school's *worst* faery?"

"How is that my fault?" Mona said, hot fury suddenly overriding her sense. "You think you're the only faery with expectations weighing on you? My *mother* is a Priestess, and she expects *me* to succeed her! You're right, I was the worst. How can a worthless faery like me be a Priestess? Don't you see? I don't want to be the best just for the sake of it; I *need* to be the best. And, finally, I feel like I *deserve* to be here!"

"You never deserved to be here," Felicia said, venom dripping from her tongue. "Your family's great fortune was quenched with your mother's disgraceful deeds."

"Don't you say anything about my mother."

"Or what?" She raised a challenging eyebrow. "It's true. She's a disgrace to Hailbrand University. We're supposed to keep the secrets of our great magic, and she went and spread it around like the stars-damned *sentimental* fool that she is, all because she couldn't take the deaths of a few *miserable* creatures." She stepped closer. "You think anyone respects her after that? The only reason she's still alive is because people fear her."

"Maybe you should," Mona said through gritted teeth. "And you should also talk about her with more respect. You might regret it otherwise."

"What, are *you* threatening me?" Felicia barked out a laugh. "Oh, that's cute. It would be one thing were it *your mother* making that threat. But you? Please, I could scorch out your soul with just a snap of my fingers." A click, and a flame sprang out in the palms of Felicia's hands, her eyes blazing a fuming red.

"Oh, yes?" Mona said, and before she could fully process what she was thinking, her mouth was saying, "Jack, take her powers!"

"What?" Felicia could only let out a confused whimper as Jack jumped out of Mona's bag and lunged at her, barbed teeth sinking into her throat.

Felicia's screams echoed in the hallway as moonlight shone through the stained glass and the first chime of midnight rang. Mona trembling hands covered her mouth as the color in Felicia's body was drained, washed down until her skin was like a gray raisin. The shrieking stopped, and the empty body fell with a heavy *thud*.

Mona couldn't mouth any words, her vision growing fuzzy. Jack went back to her, licking the blood from his teeth. Mona screamed.

"What, Master?" Jack said, startled. "Was it not to your liking?"

"What the hell was that?" Mona demanded. "You were supposed to take her powers, not *kill* her!"

"How else do you think I'd take her powers?" Jack said with a grin. "What, never seen a faery's powers wilt before?"

Mona couldn't breathe and took her hands to her throat as she gasped for air.

"Now, now, don't be alarmed," said Jack. "You have one less nuisance to worry about."

"I didn't want to kill her!"

"Didn't you? That's not what I saw in your mind."

"That's... I was... I was angry!"

"Yes, and when you're not angry, you still want her to die. Her two friends as well," Jack said. "If you ask me, she had it coming. Faery Princesses are always so ... entitled."

"Oh, no, this is bad..." Mona gripped her hair, wings buzzing nervously behind her. Felicia's corpse stared at her, and the room was suddenly too tiny and too big at the same time. "I need to get out of here..."

"Hmm, and what's going to happen when they find her body?" Jack said. "You'll be in trouble. Maybe you should order me to take more powers."

"No!" Mona shouted. "You won't take more powers!"

"Then, what are my orders?"

"Nothing! You will do *nothing*!"

"You seem to not know what our little agreement entails," Jack said, still with that unnerving smile. "You have to have orders for me, or else I'll be allowed to roam free."

"What? Since when?"

"Since always." Jack laughed. "What, did you not read the fine print? Little Mona, you have much to learn before you're Priestess. In any case, you'd better find some orders for me, or else I'll find orders for myself." His grin grew even more wicked. "And remember, it'll be all. Your. Fault."

Mona felt a shiver grip her. He could read into her; he knew what her worst fears were. He'd played her like a fiddle, and fool as she was, she'd given him her name, broke the most important rule in the Fäe realm. Oh, how could she have been so stupid? All because of her selfishness and desperation.

"Indeed, you were quite the fool." Jack laughed. "And now, you're stuck with me. So, what will it be, Mona? Do you have orders for me?"

Mona was paralyzed body and soul, but still forced a reaction. "Yes," she said. "Right now, you will get rid of Felicia's body."

"Easy," he said, and his small mouth opened into a big, spiky pit. He swallowed the body whole, and it was like nothing had happened, the marble floor pristine again and the quietness returning to the hall. "Now what?"

Mona refrained from crying, "Now, you will return from whence you came and leave me and every faery alone."

Jack laughed. And laughed. And laughed ever louder. The hall darkened, clouds covering the moon and thunder drily booming. "Oh, Mona. You just set me free…"

Thus far, Jack had looked like a fluffy, harmless creature, with only pointy teeth to hint at any deeper threat. At that moment however, he grew large, claws rising like thorns, his teeth sharpening, and his eyes turning snake-like. Ears became horns, and he grew wings that were leathery and hard.

The creature growled, and the sound went through walls.

"Don't you know what happens when you free a demon?"

"A… A demon?" Mona shrieked, springing back as "Jack" stomped in her direction, the floor shaking, "I… I told you to return to where you came from!"

"I was free where I came from," "Jack" said. "Did you think you could get rid of me that easily? Your words bound me; now they unbound me. And I have your Name!"

His laugh made the air tremble, and Mona flew down the hall. She heard the demon give chase and hastened her flight, adrenaline pumping through her veins. Opening a door, she went in quickly.

"Mona… Where are you… You can't hide forever… I *own* you!"

"Mona? What is going on?" She'd entered Miss Dahlia's classroom, and there her professor was, kind, round face creased in nerves.

"Miss Dahlia!" Mona flew to her. "We have to evacuate the school! A demon is running loose!"

"A demon? Mona, what did you do?"

"I accidentally summoned a demon, and…"

"How did you summon a demon *accidentally*?"

"There's no time to explain!" Mona shouted, hearing the rumble of faery screams and demonic laughter. "Please, help me!"

"So, this is how you improved so much." Miss Dahlia shook her head. "I am so disappointed in you, Mona."

Mona's stomach dropped, but she wasn't surprised. "I promise I'll leave the school *after* we deal with the demon!"

That was when the wall to the classroom came crumbling down, and both Mona and Miss Dahlia lost their balance. Dust crawled into Mona's eyes and lungs.

"There you are!" the demon's voice resounded. "And you're with that annoying professor of yours. Good. It'll be amazing to make you watch as I devour her."

"Mona!" Miss Dahlia screamed as a scaly tentacle burst from the demon's tummy and crawled around her waist, pulling her directly into its gargantuan mouth.

"Miss Dahlia!" Tears flowed freely down Mona's cheeks, and her throat hurt from screaming.

"Oh, isn't it sweet. You really cared about this old hag," the demon mocked and stepped closer. Mona could hardly breathe, tasting vomit on her tongue and feeling her head so light and heavy that she could faint. She was lost, stranded in an island.

She needed her mother.

"Mommy can't save you, sweetheart," the demon said. "You want to know how to put an end to this?"

"How?" Mona said, rage and sorrow alight in her eyes, "How do I stop you? I already gave you my name, what else do you want?"

"Your powers."

"What?"

"You heard me."

"What powers? Everything I did was because of you!"

"It's truly unfortunate that such great magic should be granted to a fool like you," the demon said. "Your mother was right. You have immense powers you haven't even begun to tap into. What I made you able to do is only a fraction of what you're capable of. It's wasted on you. Give. It. To. Me."

The demon stepped closer, and Mona retreated, back against the wall. If what the demon was saying was true, then she couldn't give up her powers. What else could happen to the school, or the world? How could she stop this, what could she do?

<My sweet dear,> her mother's voice suddenly echoed in her mind. *<Don't reply, the demon can't know I'm here. Listen closely: to vanquish the demon, you will have to find its True Name. Look into the True Realm. Don't stray. Watch where he's standing. Focus and be calm. Once you find it, speak it and send him away.>*

Mona closed her eyes. She could hear the demon approach, but her mother's soothing voice was like a blanket protecting her from the coldest of nights.

In the True Realm, the moon's chimes rang louder, but every voice was distant and softer. The shadows were clearer now thanks to the demon's magic, and Mona hurried to look for its shape. She always felt off-kilter when she traveled to the True Realm, so she fought harder to ground herself. Miss Dahlia's class was to the east. The demon had come from the left, the southern part. She searched the shapes there, recognizing the Names of the board, the chairs, the desks, and the scattered books that fell from the broken shelves.

A small, floating thing rumbled in the air, and letters were revolving around it. She approached and touched them, struggling to Know their order. She thought of its earthly form, how it hid such a small, frail essence. A shield to cover a ball of glass. Its True Form shook and quivered as it tried to face her with every strength it possessed, stripped of its heavy, menacing mantle.

Suddenly, the Name was clear.

What happens when you find a True Name?
One hardly ever ponders this question.

You speak it, gain power over it, and morph reality
to your will.

But no one truly knows the full power of a Name.

If you happen to learn the True Name of one of
this world's shadows, will you speak it?

Mother Drauga

By Kay Hanifen

Drauga was getting worried. The sun was slowly sinking over the horizon, and all children were accounted for but one: Mira. Sweet Mira, with hair of spun gold and eyes that held an ocean of wit and intelligence within. She was growing older, and with her age came more responsibilities in caring for the rest of Drauga's orphans. So, she had sent the girl down to the village to pick up the prosthetic leg that Drauga had commissioned for one of her boys, Yelen, who had shot up in height this year.

Mira could be trusted. Drauga knew this. The girl was clever, witty, and occasionally mischievous, but she was reliable. If she asked her to get something done, it would be accomplished quickly and efficiently.

Still, mothers are nothing if not worriers, and she'd been gone for hours. Maybe Mira got busy chatting with someone she liked. She was getting to the age where she might find a partner and marry. A part of Drauga hoped that Mira preferred women to men. Her children who fell in love with someone of the same sex were more likely to stay and help her with the rest of her hoard of orphans. More importantly though, she would miss Mira when she left. Drauga didn't play favorites, but there was something about this child that made her think that she would do great things.

"Mother?" One of her younger children tugged on a wing, trying to get her attention.

She tore her gaze from the mouth of the cave that they called home. "What is it, Kiov?" she asked, affectionately nosing him.

He giggled and staggered at the weight of her nudge. "When is dinner? I'm starving."

"When Mira returns," she replied, worrying her tail between her front claws, an old nervous habit. She wanted to believe her daughter was running late, but a mother knows when something is wrong, the pit in her stomach telling her that Mira was somehow in danger. This instinct had saved many of her children over the years, letting her catch illnesses early and rescue any wayward orphans who had been injured while playing, so she'd learned to listen to it. "On second thought, I'll go looking for her." Raising her voice, she called, "Lor, Sava, come here please."

Lor was busy teaching some of the younger children reading and writing, while Sava cooked. When they heard her call, both dropped what they were doing and approached.

"What is it, Mother?" Sava asked.

At eighteen and nineteen respectively, these were the oldest of her children, so she relied on them the most when she was not there. It rarely happened, but they had proven themselves more than capable in the past. "I'm going out looking for Mira," she said. "Hopefully I'll be back within the hour, but until I return, you two are in charge. Give the rest of the children supper and put them to bed if I don't return by then. Try to keep to the routine like usual, and I'll be back with your wayward sister soon."

Lor wrapped his arms around her neck and squeezed. "Be safe out there, Mother."

She nudged him affectionately. "And you do the same, loves." Raising her voice, she announced to the rest of her hoard that she was leaving and that Lor and Sava would be in charge. Once she was sure that the rest of the children understood, she stepped out of the cave, unfurled her wings, and leapt off the face of the sheer cliff that she had made her home centuries ago.

It felt better to be moving, to pump her wings and gain momentum. Moving always feels better than waiting... Even when you aren't truly going forward like you want. That was the danger of it. There is a time for movement and there is a time for patience, so she forced herself to go slow, retracing the route her children had been taking to the village for the past several centuries.

Every dragon had a hoard. The stereotype was that they coveted gold and jewels—and many did—but that wasn't the only thing they collected. Some hoarded books, others hoarded quilts, and she'd even met some dragons that hoarded cats and chickens. Because she could have no pups of her own, she hoarded human children, taking in and raising the orphaned and the unwanted until they were ready to spread their metaphorical wings and fly. Many chose to stay close though, often becoming pillars of the neighboring villages and visiting her on occasion.

Because she was so much longer lived than the humans she raised, she had seen plenty of death, but she grieved them all. The easiest ones were those that died of old age. They had lived long, happy lives, and were inevitably surrounded by loved ones. Those that died in the prime of their lives—usually in childbirth or from an injury or illness—were harder for her to grieve. They had lived well, but fate cut their lives too short. The most devastating, though, were the children in her care that died. It wasn't often. She did everything in her power to keep them safe and healthy, but mothers frequently left sickly babies and toddlers at the mouth of her cave in a last-ditch attempt to save them, and children had a habit of getting into trouble and hurting themselves. Sometimes, there was just no saving them.

Mira had been one of those sickly children abandoned at the mouth of her cave, and there was a time that Drauga wasn't sure that she would survive their first winter together. She spent many sleepless nights keeping her warm, making sure she was fed, and holding her close. Mira came out of her fever deaf in one ear, but so full of life that it spilled out from her, invigorating others with her mere presence. Sweet, bold Mira, who climbed the highest trees and made the children laugh when they were frightened. Drauga prayed that she was safe.

Smoke billowed up from the nearest village, and she landed, her stomach already in knots as she took in the empty houses. The normally lively town was eerily silent. Signs of fighting littered the ground: swords, shields, arrows, and the occasional body. Raiders had attacked suddenly and only burned down one of the buildings, apparently more interested in the people than wanton destruction.

But Mira was not among the dead. Some of the tension bled from her body at that realization, but not much. Mira was not dead. But if she didn't find her soon, she might suffer a fate worse than death. Drauga would not let that happen. If the raiders so much as harmed a hair on her head, she would lay waste to them and feast on their flesh. Taking to the sky once more, she circled overhead, searching for any signs of camp. Laden with prisoners as they were, they couldn't have gotten that far, even if they took the nearby river to escape.

The river. All the boats were gone, commandeered by these monsters. When she landed, she found more signs of them having been there. Footprints littered the mud and sand, and all the boats' moorings had been cut. Flicking out her tongue in search of any signs of her missing child, she tasted the air. Her children all smelled slightly of sulfur, a byproduct of living with a dragon and unique to their family.

There. Sulfur and a touch of sawdust. She had been to the woodcrafter before the attack happened. Drauga followed the smell until she reached a small holly bush. Judging by the way the ground had been disturbed, someone had been sitting or lying there.

Then, Drauga became aware of another smell. Blood. It came from the holly bush, the evening breeze carrying the odor along with a flicker of movement. A small blue ribbon had been caught on the branches. A ribbon much like the one Mira wore on her way to the village earlier today. She carefully extricated it and realized two things with a start: that it was the source of the blood and that something had been written with it.

DS

Drauga smiled, a feeling of pride welling like the fire in her chest. Her clever, clever girl. As the full moon began to rise, she took to the air once more.

There was a time when Mira was excited to go to the village on her own. It meant that Mother trusted her with responsibilities befitting her age, and she had no intention of letting her down.

Sitting on the raiders' boat, though, she struggled to believe that it was only this morning that she'd leapt out of bed, raced to get dressed, scarfed down breakfast, and nearly forgot her favorite blue ribbon to tie up her golden hair. The ribbon was one of the only things she had from her birth mother, and as much as she loved Mother Drauga, holding it made her feel like she was with the mother she never got to know.

It was only one errand that she needed to run, but Mother always gave her a little extra so she could buy herself lunch and a treat while there. With a dagger concealed up her sleeve for protection, she practically skipped down the mountain, already imagining the taste of sweetberry bread and the new book she would buy to share with the rest of her family, after reading it herself, of course; that was the rule for anyone who used the extra coin Mother gave them to buy books.

The woodcrafter's shop was on the outskirts of town, and she hummed a silly little tune as she approached. Stupid Farthy, one of the older orphans of the hoard, said that she was a bad singer, but Mira didn't care. She knew Mother only took Farthy in because the village couldn't stand her smell, anyway.

Mr. Nimar, the woodcrafter, was busy in his workshop when she entered. He set aside his hammer when he saw her, a twinkle in his eyes as he tapped his nose. "You're one of Drauga's kids, right?"

She nodded. "Mother commissioned a wooden leg for my hoardmate, Yelen."

The woodcrafter nodded. "It's in the back. Just a moment, please."

Tapping her foot, she danced from side to side, eager for this chore to be over so she could have some fun on the village proper. The door opened again, and some unfamiliar men in pile-woven wool cloaks entered. Something about those men unsettled her. They stood tense, coiled like snakes about to strike, their hands hovering over their weapons. One of them looked to be about her age. He kept leering at her, studying her like a piece of meat and making her feel inexplicably ashamed.

Craning her neck, she tried to find Mr. Nimar in the back. After another tense, agonizing minute, he reappeared holding the wooden leg. When he saw their new guests, he froze, his eyes wide. "Who are you?"

And that's when the screaming started. Though Mira's ears were not quite as good as others', even she could hear the sounds of battle and terror emanating from the outside. The leader of the men grinned wolfishly, his hand resting on the pommel of his sword, ready to draw it the moment she or Mr. Nimar made one wrong move. "Please, we have very little," Mr. Nimar begged. "Have mercy."

"It depends," he said. "We've heard rumors of a dragon in the area with an extensive hoard, *and* that you've recently had dealings with it. Tell us where to find it, and we won't kill you all."

"She comes to me. I don't know where to find her," he said, which was half true. Most knew where to leave any unwanted or orphaned infants and children, but very few braved the climb aside from the cunning women who lived deep in the woods.

"I don't believe you," the leader replied, and with a silent signal, the men drew their weapons.

"I can help you," she squeaked before she could think better of it. The men stared at her incredulously, save for Mr. Nimar, who looked somewhere between shocked and horrified. Mira continued, "If you let the people of this village go, I'll show you where you can find the dragon you seek."

The boy her age scoffed. "You? What would you know of dragons?"

She put her hands on her hips. "More than you." Pulling out her purse, she dumped the contents onto the table Mr. Nimar used for his transactions. It wasn't like she was getting books or sweetberry bread anyway. "Where do you think I got this coin? I know where its hoard is."

The men gasped, their eyes widening at the gold she carried with her. Though Mother hoarded children, she was not above collecting wealth. That said, most of it belonged to her own mother and was gifted to her so that she could support her ever growing family. Mira had never met Grandmother Kyaja. The dragon had decided to go into a decades-long hibernation shortly before she was born, but the older kids who remembered Grandmother spoke fondly of her. Mother was unusually generous for a dragon, and cheerily parted with her gold if it meant making her children happy.

These raiders wouldn't care, though, that this dragon raised orphans with as much love as any birth parent could give. No, they only cared for the wealth, which meant that Mira had to protect her family from them. "Let everyone else go, and I'll take you to it," she repeated.

The leader grinned. "A compromise, perhaps." Two of the men approached Mr. Nimar while the boy and another man approached her, their weapons glinting in the morning light. The boy held his knife to her throat, standing so close that she could smell his rank breath. The leader cupped her cheek in the parody of a familiar gesture. "Lead me to the dragon, and I'll let these villagers live as slaves. Refuse, and we'll kill you all where you stand."

She swallowed. A whole village would be harder for Mother to rescue than just her, but not impossible. "Agreed."

He stepped back. "Ulf, bind her and take her to the river while we round up the rest."

"Yes, Father." As he tied her arms in front of her, he leaned in close and whispered, "If you're good, I'll make you my bride."

Mira resisted the urge to spit on him. If she wanted to survive long enough for her mother to find her, she had to be clever. As they walked to the docks, she made a mental inventory of what she had: a small knife, barely useful in a fight; a hair ribbon, also useless; the clothes on her back; and the other captives. And her mother. She didn't have to fight the raiders off to escape. That wouldn't be necessary. All she had to do was keep them distracted until her mother found her. But how would Mother know where she was?

The ribbon.

Ulf sat her down away from the other prisoners. She supposed she was now too important for them to risk her somehow sparking a rebellion and escaping. All they saw was a girl with no muscles on her too-small body and the fighting experience of a gnat, but they were being somewhat careful.

They had posted a guard on her, but he was inattentive, seeming to prefer staring into space or chatting with his fellow raiders than babysitting a thirteen-year-old. She let out a sob that was only partially a performance and curled herself into a ball. Keeping an eye on her guard to make sure he wasn't paying attention, she untied the ribbon from her hair. Sitting up, she concealed it in her sleeve until she was sure her sobs were being ignored.

Turning her back to him, she used her teeth to pull down the sleeve that concealed her knife. She bit down on the soft leather of the pommel and pulled the blade free, taking it with her dominant hand. Then, she pulled out the ribbon. Now, for the hard part. Biting her lip to keep from crying out from the pain, she sliced into her pointer finger. A bead of blood formed, and she used it to write *DS* on the ribbon. Mother would figure out that she meant downstream. She was smart like that.

After concealing the ribbon in a nearby holly bush, she got to work cutting the rope binding her. She was careful to only weaken it, leaving a few woven strands so that it would still stay together. Otherwise, she risked them discovering the blade.

Carefully, she slid the knife back into its sheath on her gauntlet. Now all she could do was wait and cry until Mother came. By her estimation, Mother would become worried when she hadn't returned before dark. The raiders were busy at the moment, their arms laden with their spoils and swarming the boats like ants. The people would be the last to board. It was easier to guard them on land. If they were in the boat, then some might jump into the water in a desperate bid to escape and likely drown in the process. At least on land, they could be chased down.

It might take an hour or two for them to load the boats with their stolen goods and then a few minutes more to drag the people on board. At the moment, the sun was high in the sky, and given that it was mid-spring, there was probably about seven hours of daylight left. A five-hour head start on a boat working with the current. Maybe she should have said upstream, but that would have brought them closer to Mother and the rest of the hoard, which was the last thing she wanted. At least this way if Mother couldn't find her, she and the rest of the family would be safe.

All she could do now was wait.

She listened to the men as they talked, picking up on the fact that the leader was Ulf's father, a warrior named Ragnar. They had come from the islands up north in search of treasure, and this was the boy's first raid. After about two hours—judging by the sun's position in the sky—they loaded her onto the ship with the rest of the raiders rather than the one containing the prisoners.

The ones who were not in Mr. Nimar's workshop stared at her with open curiosity. Mira kept her back straight and her head held high, just like Mother taught her to. All her life, people who weren't a part of the hoard would stare and whisper when they saw her. Mira Draugasdotter. Mira, daughter of the dragon. She did her best to make Mother proud by ignoring the stares and commanding respect, while also treating others the way she wanted to be treated. The stares of these raiders were no different.

"How far downstream do we go?" Ragnar asked.

Mira squinted at the horizon, trying to figure out the best route to slow them. She considered sending them towards the rapids or waterfall, but that risked the lives of the villagers on the other ship. No, that would not do. It was better to just go straight. Mother was more likely to find her on a direct route. Raising both hands, she pointed straight downstream. "Ten miles that way, I think. I usually walk there through the forest."

"You think," Ulf scoffed. She was really beginning to hate the boy. He was broad shouldered and brutish, apparently more brawn than brain.

"My feet have memorized the land better than any map," she retorted. "It's that way. Her cave is near the river."

Ragnar nodded. "I am choosing to trust you. If I discover that you've lied to me, you will learn a new definition of the word pain. Am I understood?"

She swallowed, her mouth going dry as he gave the rest a signal to set sail. For most of the journey, she sat in silence aside from occasionally reassuring them that they were going in the right direction.

"There's something I don't understand," Ulf said as the sky began to turn red.

The old poem sprang to mind:
Red sky at night, sailor's delight.
Red sky at morning, sailors take warning.

He leaned casually against the mast where she sat and nudged her. "I asked you a question."

"No, you didn't. You just made a comment, so I assumed that not understanding anything was simply a statement of fact." She didn't feel the slap, not at first. As someone raised around nearly thirty other siblings, she was used to occasionally being hit, but those were never done with the intent to cause true pain. Stars danced in front of her eyes. Her cheek stung, and red poured down her nose.

He looked down at her with an infuriatingly smug grin. "Why don't you try that again?"

"What don't you understand?" she gritted out.

"Sir." He was enjoying this, the sadistic prick.

"What don't you understand, sir?"

"Why the wooden leg? Both of yours seem to be functioning fine."

This? Not the fact that she seems to know a dragon? Very well, she had an easy answer for this question. "It's for my brother. He lost his leg to gangrene as a child."

He studied her for a moment before shrugging, apparently accepting this answer. A flicker of movement in the sky caught her eye and she grinned. Ulf looked over his shoulder, apparently trying to follow her gaze. "What are you grinning about?"

"My mother knows I'm missing. She's going to be very displeased by your people and the way you treated me," she said, this time giving him a smug grin.

Ulf scoffed. "Why should I care about the pleasure of a single crone?"

There were shouts from behind him as Mother descended, and he turned around in time to see her land on the boat with a *thud* powerful enough to shake it. Her red-and-black scales shimmered like embers in the late evening sun, and smoke billowed from her flared nostrils. She scanned the crowd for a moment, and then her gaze settled on Mira. Some of the tension relaxed from her body, but not much. She was still on a boat full of battle-hardened humans.

Mira flashed Ulf a grin and broke the rope binding her with ease as she got to her feet. "Perhaps you should care. Because *that* is my mother."

Drauga could have wept with relief when she saw Mira. Her little girl was alive, but judging by the smell of her blood and the red dripping down her nose, she was not wholly unhurt. These men *hurt* her daughter.

She was not a fighter. She had not joined in any wars and was too popular among the locals for any errant knights to be directed to her doorstep. On the rare occasion that she did get into a fight, she often erred on the side of mercy. Not today. Not with her daughter taken and bleeding.

The raiders drew their weapons and charged. It may as well have been children playfighting with sticks. The swords and axes did little to pierce her armor of scales, and she knocked the men aside like wooden toy soldiers. Biting the head off one, she spat it out before grabbing another by the chest, crushing it in her massive jaws like a peanut in its shell. This only served to enrage the others.

Good.

She was enraged too, so much so that she could feel the flames forming inside her. With a roar, she let it out, the smell of cooked pork filling the air. Those that did not die fled the ship, including a boy that looked to be about Mira's age.

Mira.

The girl, having taken shelter on the bow of the ship, clung to the wooden dragon's head. She was not a strong swimmer, so she was reluctant to jump into the water. Unfurling her wings, Drauga flew to her, scooping her up and carrying her to shore.

Setting her down, she examined her, gently running her claws up and down in search of broken bones and serious wounds. "Are you hurt, Mira? I smell your blood."

She wrinkled her injured nose. "I'm fine, Mother. A nosebleed and a pricked finger won't kill me."

Drauga relaxed just a little. "I'm glad you're safe."

But then Mira looked behind her. "What about the other villagers? They were on the boat behind us."

And indeed, she could see them chained and huddled together. They were friends to her, so it was her turn to be friends to them. Taking off, she made quick work of the guards on that boat, this time having enough self-control to avoid setting it on fire.

Once all the raiders were dead or had fled, she broke their chains.

"Thank you," the head of the village said as they got to work changing course and rowing upstream. "We owe you a debt."

Drauga smiled. "It's the least I can do after all you've done to help me."

Once she was sure that they were on their way home, Drauga returned to her daughter. Mira sat, shaking, by the shore, the stress of the day finally hitting her as she threw herself into Drauga's arms and sobbed.

"What happened, love?" Drauga asked. "Why were you on a different boat than the rest?"

"They wanted to kill you," she cried.

Drauga blinked. That, she had not expected. "Me?"

"For your hoard. They wanted all your gold and would probably take the rest of us as slaves or worse, so I acted like I was going to take them to you so that they wouldn't kill anyone else, but I was really leading them away, and..."

Drauga hushed her, a feeling of pride glowing in her chest, though tempered a bit by the terror of what happened that day and what might have happened if it all went wrong. Mira risked her own life and freedom to keep the village alive and her family safe. If Drauga hadn't gotten there in time, she could have lost her forever. But if Mira hadn't gone with the raiders, the village likely would've been massacred, and they would have eventually found their way to Drauga's home. "You were very brave to protect us like that. My clever little girl. I'm so proud of you."

At that, Mira sobbed harder, and Drauga held her until all the tears had been rung out of her body, and her fear had been replaced by exhaustion. Scooping the sleeping Mira in her arms, Drauga unfurled her wings and flew them home.

A Fisherman's Tail

by Valerie Willis

The peach-colored sun had broken away from the purple horizon when Tad made it to the fishing pier. Every fisherman in the region knew the best spot was at the far end where the water looked like the blackest pitch. It was impossible to weasel in between the old timers who claimed the railing at the tip of the dock. In fact, it was considered a rite of passage to fish among those fishing gurus. The old men were never satisfied with their catch, despite how large or plentiful.

Tad and the younger newcomers joked on occasion about how they never left the pier, as if immortally soul bound to the old, rickety pier. One time, he thought he would get himself a spot, braving to go down the pier during a bad storm. Salt stung his eyes and nostrils, waves knocking him down to his knees. Much to his horror, the old men were all there, fishing on as if the waves splashing over them were a summer's breeze.

Snorting, he thought, *Today, that is going to change!* He started marching down the wooden appendage, his steps echoing, bouncing the whole way. He was determined to elbow his way between two of the old skin-and-bone entities for a chance to gain a good round of fishing. At the rate he was catching, he earned enough fish to feed himself and pay for his bait, nothing more. Drawing near, he tightened his grip on his pole and bait bucket.

Stumbling to a stop, he blinked; one of the five fishing gurus was missing. Rubbing his eyes, he stared at the empty corner on the right side, astonished. Walking up to the railing, he held his breath as they all turned to take notice of him.

"Well look at this, boys!" chuckled the bristly faced man next to him. "We've got ourselves a replacement."

The man next to him, the middle fishing sage, whistled, "Ain't he pretty."

"Not for long!" shouted the tallest one at the opposite corner.

This sent the quartet of smelly, greasy, unshaven old men into a roar of laughter.

"Shush, Gerald!" warned the man next to the tall one. "Let the boy fish."

"All right," sighed Gerald.

"What you fishing for?" The man middle in the middle of the group lifted an eyebrow. "Dogfish? Grouper? Maybe snapper even?"

Tad smirked, deciding to appeal to their humor. "A wife."

Another roar of laughter assured he had succeeded.

"Oh, he's a keeper." The man next to him slowed his laughter, catching his breath. "The name's Jedidiah."

"Tad, sir." He tilted his cap to them all. "It's an honor to get to fish next to such well-respected men."

Jedidiah elbowed the middle man. "You hear that, Jeff?"

"Yea, I heard it." He snorted, a scowl on his face. "I wouldn't exactly call us that."

Tad blinked. "By the way, what happened to the man who normally fishes this corner?"

"He's dead," sighed Gerald at the opposite corner. "Not sure what killed him, but when he fell over the railing..."

"Yea, he went over too fast for Jed to catch 'im," added the man next to Gerald. "I'm Lester. In case you haven't caught their names, this tall one in the corner to my left is Gerald, Jeff in the center there, Old Jed next to ya. We're harmless. Just old and tired, that's all."

"Nice to meet you all..." Feeling unnerved knowing they let their longtime friend fall over into the black abyss below, he focused on fishing.

As he baited his hook with a shrimp and cast it out into the deep unknown, he couldn't help but notice the look on the old fishermen's faces. Joining them, he too leaned on the railing, staring at them in curiosity. They were all wrinkled from the sun, weathered and beaten with their unshaven chins. The most disturbing thing was that the glazed look in their eyes had so easily returned to them after their introduction. Often, he and the other boys had tried to talk to these totems of fishing with no luck or advice. A chill made him shudder despite the heat from the sun beginning to sting at his face. Something about these old men seemed like a fairytale.

Did they only speak to me in order to secure a fifth man at the end of the pier? Staring at his line, it ceased to be seen past where it connected to the top of the water. *What happens when I pack up and leave? Will someone take my place? Or am I expected to stay in a never-ending loop of fishing for all eternity?*

Gerald's posture shifted and he stood taller, pulling the line on his reel. Tad watched the old man's eyes start to shine, a brilliant blue full of life. Adrenaline washing away his sleepy demeanor, Gerald positioned his hands on his rod ever so carefully. He yanked up; it was a strong and seamless motion, and Tad felt himself in awe watching Gerald set the hook. The long, sleek, flimsy wood bent over as if it were wrapping around an invisible barrel. He reeled and pulled, reeled and pulled; leaning first one way, then the other. The fight was on!

The rest watched on, amazed by the struggle between man and fish. Gerald pushed into Lester, which led to the bulk of them smashing Tad into the corner. Then Gerald stumbled back to his corner, planting a heel on the railing, pulling the rod high. The tip of the rod bent over, folding in half from the feat. Gerald grunted, another round of reel and pull; he was desperate to make the fish tired enough to bring it to the pier.

"What in the hell do you got?" marveled Jeff.

"Not sure," rumbled Gerald, managing to reel in more line. "Oh! I see a flash of gold!"

"Gold?" Tad knotted his brow. "What sort of fish is gold in color?"

Splish! Splish-splash!

The fish had breached. They all leaned far over the railing to get a shot at seeing the fish Gerald was tugging up to the deck. Tad pulled his hat off, glaring at the shiny finned treasure. As it plopped down at Gerald's feet, they all gasped in wonder. The fish was large, maybe a good fifty pounds, plump and round with long flowing fins. The most amazing feature was its golden scales. They glimmered in the sunlight like thousands of coins.

"Hot dog, boys! I caught myself a goldfish!" Gerald was doing a little jig in celebration, "Now I can pay off my debts so my wife will let me back in the house! I'm going home, boys!"

No one spoke a word, still stunned by the golden wonder as it opened and closed its mouth at them. Grabbing a worn-out sailor's jacket, Gerald wrapped his treasure so none of it could be seen. He took two steps but paused, turning to the rest of his fishing compadres.

With tears in his eyes, he wished them a farewell, "May Lady Luck be kind to you."

"Aye," mumbled Lester.

There were only four men at the end of the pier, and to Tad, it felt like a gaping hole. None of the younger men nearby seemed to take notice of a chance to get one of the best spots. Huffing, Tad bobbed his rod, feeling no signs of a bite or even a snag on the line. Sighing, he watched the men to his left, his interest growing. Lester's brow was folding, his mouth twisting; he tugged the line, reeled it in a little, then snorted.

"Dang, I think I got a wad of weeds on it again," Lester's rod was bent over with the weight of the debris, but it lacked the fight Gerald's had shown.

Tad watched him reeling in his line. As the end of the line reached the top of the water, his eyes grew wide to see something red and green sparkling in the sunlight. Lester also looked confused, reeling faster, curiosity goading him to hurry. Pulling it over the railing, it became clear what he had managed to retrieve from the unknown. Tangled in his fishing line was a mermaid's purse. Rubies studded the entire outer shell of what would have been a shark's egg case, with green silken straps imitating seaweed. The accessory was beyond gorgeous, even to an old fisherman's eyes.

Lester whistled, "Woo-wee! Ain't my wife going to be head over heels for something this fancy!"

"I've never seen anything like that before..." breathed Jeff, the fisherman who used to be in the center.

"Me neither." Jed rubbed his jaw. "What you gonna do with it, Lester?"

"Give it to the wife!" He gave Jed an expression as if he had been asked a stupid question. "I can go home with this in my hands! She's always whining I never get her anything nice, and here, boys, is my ticket!"

That being said, he abandoned his fishing gear. Tad watched Lester run full-steam down the pier with a tight grip on the red-and-green treasure. All three of them looked to one another with a sigh. What once was five fishermen at the end of the pier was now three. Jeff shuffled himself over between where Gerald and Lester had been.

"Wonder what else is down there..." He winked at Jedidiah and Tad.

They watched Jeff bait his hook, check the weights one more time, and with a groan, he gave it the best cast he could. The reel let its line flow fast and loose, with only Jeff's fingertips gauging how slow the weights fell through the unseen depths. Jeff flipped the lever, bringing the line to a halt. He tugged the rod once, then twice. Looking over, Tad locked eyes with Jeff, who smiled with a twinkle in his eye. With a hard yank, Jeff attempted to set the hook.

"Shoot!" he fussed, stomping his foot. "And I bet I threw my bait off as hard as I yanked that sucker!"

Jedidiah laughed. "Got too excited thinking you'd catch something like Gerald or Lester, huh?"

"You hush your mouth," snorted Jeff, reeling the line in.

Tad leaned against the railing, still no bites or signs of anything taking interest in his own line. Perhaps this seemed like a good spot to fish due to its occupants rarely leaving. Sighing, he watched the waves roll in, slurping and smacking into the pylons below. A flash of white caught his attention, his heart racing for a second before he realized it was Jeff's line. Squinting, he saw it break water. He realized there was something long and sparkling caught on the hook and weights.

"What is tangled in your line, Jeff?" Tad stood tall, watching the lump fall at Jeff's feet.

"Well, I'll be a monkey's uncle..." whispered Jeff. "It's a pearl necklace."

"And a long one, at that," added Jedidiah.

Jeff untangled the necklace and rolled it between his fingers. Not satisfied they were real, he placed a pearl in his mouth, lightly biting his teeth on it. His eyes grew wide as he looked back at the thirty-inch necklace. After a moment, he turned his eyes back to Jed and Tad.

"They're... they're real!" He shoved them in his pocket. "My old lady always nags me about not getting her jewelry. This ought to do the trick to get me back in the door!"

Grabbing his pole, Jeff left the two of them behind. Looking to one another, Tad wasn't sure what to think about the events the day had brought. Only one fishing guru remained.

"Does this happen often?" he questioned Jedidiah.

"Never…" He shook his head, sliding down to give the two of them more space. "Let's hope we are as lucky as the rest of the boys."

"Let's hope!" said Tad, nodding with enthusiasm.

Reeling up his line, he found no bait on his hook.

"Fishing on credit, I see," snickered Jedidiah.

"Yea…" Tad added another shrimp and sent his line back to the sea. "Good luck to us both."

Jedidiah nodded in agreement. They both fell back into the sleepy state of waiting. The sun was falling at their backsides, two hours shy of connecting with the horizon. Again, no bites, no nibbles tapped on Tad's line. The water below them was growing ever darker, more menacing with the fading sunlight.

Reeeeeeeeeeeee!

Jedidiah's reel screamed, making them jolt back to life. His line was taut, his reel failing to slow the fish down. Jed fumbled to click the button, upping the drag until the reel could hold fast. He pulled and reeled, pulled and reeled. Jed stumbled backwards, putting his weight into the fight. The reel clicked and whined on occasion as the fish fought back. Sweat was dripping off Jed's chin, the old man panting as his arms shook.

Looking over to Tad, he was panicking. "I'm gonna need your help to lug this one in!"

Tad rushed to his side, gripping the pole with Jed. The old man sighed, happy to get some reprieve. The tugging on the line made the pole wiggle and dance in their grip. The strength of the beast was startling. Tad realized Jed had backed away from the railing in fear of being pulled over. Whatever he had, it was fast and large. An hour had passed as they worked together to pull, then lean forward to reel, which led into another strong pull. One last tug from them and they felt the fish's will to fight dissipate and allowed the line to drag him closer to the pier. They reeled in the unknown behemoth, eager to see what Jed had caught. Approaching the railing with caution at the sound of splashing, Tad leaned over, shocked to see Jedidiah had hooked a monstrous fish.

"What is it?" Jed was still reeling in the slack. "What did I hook into?"

"It's... it's a giant seahorse!" Tad ran for his gear; he knew he had an old rope somewhere. "We're gonna need to rope him to get him up and over, or the line might snap!"

Rushing back to the railing, he made a slipknot at one end. Skillfully, he managed to land the loop over the tail of the panting orange-and-chestnut beast. Putting a foot in the railing, he leaned his weight into the rope, leveraging the seahorse up. It took all their strength to grab the man-sized creature and roll it up and over the railing. All three fell onto the dock.

Light burst from the seahorse when it hit the wooden deck. Before their eyes, the seahorse shifted into a massive chestnut-colored horse. He had thick, heavy muscles and a long orange mane and tail. It snorted and whinnied at Jedidiah as if to acknowledge the old man had earned the title of being his owner. Blinking, Tad was floored to have seen so many miracles caught off the end of the pier. Looking over to Jed, Tad saw that he had climbed to his feet and was dancing.

"It's a miracle!" Jed threw his hat off. "I got myself a horse!"

"I had heard fairytales, but this..." Tad was at a loss for words.

"This here, boy, is my chance to quell my wife's fussing!" He removed the rope from the tail and unhooked the horse's mouth. "I'll be able to plow the fields again!"

Blinking, Tad questioned, "Your wife?"

The old man put the roped around the horse's muzzle. "You mind if I take this rope?"

"N... no..." Tad stood up, watching Jedidiah leaving in a hurry, leaving him with many questions.

Looking to the end of the pier, there was nothing but leftover fishing gear from the fishing gurus. Determined to keep at it, he decided to check his line. Again, his bait was missing. Moving to the center of the railing, he hooked on another shrimp. With all his strength, he cast his line as far out as he could. At his back, the sun was setting, daylight turning into a burning pink-and-purple color. He replayed the day in his head over and over. Every fishing tale his father ever told him had come to life there before him. His mind wondered if the last tale about the fisherman's wife was true, *was she really...*

A tug on his line broke his thoughts. He leaned over the railing, peering down at the water where his line dove deep. Another tug sent his heart racing, adrenaline pumping. He waited for a hard bite. A glow started emanating from under his line. It grew brighter, larger, and then his breath caught in his throat. A woman's face emerged next to his line, her eyes brilliant blue, her golden hair glowing, her lips red, and below her, swished a lovely green-and-purple mermaid's tail. Swallowing, he leaned harder over the railing as she waved up at Tad. He pointed to himself, and she smiled and nodded.

"H... how can I help you?" stuttered Tad, leaning his pole on the railing.

"Is this your line?" She tugged on it, making the tip of his pole bend.

"Y... yes," he answered.

"You have some wonderful shrimp!" She blushed, her red cheeks bright against her pale skin. "What on earth do you do different?"

"I salt them..." he confessed.

"What is your name, kind sir?" Her voice was sweet, like an angel singing in a choir.

"T... Tad..." He was still in shock from the sight of her.

"Tad, I am in need of your help." She frowned. "My money, my purse, my necklace, even my horse, have all been stolen!"

Grimacing, he knew where it had all gone.

"If you can return them to me," she batted her long lashes, "I will gladly become your wife."

Tad paled, a shiver rattling through him. Grabbing up his pole, he reeled in his line, grabbed his gear and started to walk away.

"Wait! Tad!" she shouted after him. "Are you retrieving my items?"

Looking over, his face stern, he responded, "No, I'm quitting. After today, the last thing I want is a wife." Walking away, he mumbled under his breath, "I think I'll take that job at the castle stables I was offered last week..."

Book Club Questions

1. Which story was your favorite and why?

2. If you had to live in the world created in any of these stories, which one would you most like to live in? Which one would you hate to live in?

3. Which character(s) from any of the stories do you relate to the most?

4. If you were to write your own fantasy short story, which fantastical creature would you incorporate in it? If you would not have any creatures, what kind of fantasy trope would you write about instead?

5. If you had to fight (physically or intellectually) any of the creatures in these stories, which ones do you think you could win against? Which ones do you think you would have no chance against?

6. Would you be willing to sacrifice yourself to The Wall knowing that your sacrifice would bring light and safety back to the kingdom?

7. How would you react knowing your money at the bank was guarded by a dragon?

8. Would you eat the Galen's fruit? Do you think you would have been stuck there, or would you escape?

9. If you went fishing for an expensive accessory, what would you want to catch?

10. If you were to be raised by any kind of mythical creature, what creature would you want? Are there any that you think would be bad parents?

11. Would you want a Little Helper to do you bidding? If you did, what would you have it do?

12. Would you collect offerings for Erolkin every year if you were cursed, or would you refuse and continue your life without giving offerings?

13. Would you sacrifice yourself for the sake of a family member?

14. Do you think that it is necessary to leave your hometown to find happiness?

Editor Bio

Isabelle Reynolds is the quality control and editing intern at 4 Horsemen Publications. A native-born Cincinnatian and a recent graduate of the University of Cincinnati in history and classics, she is excited to start her new career as an editor. She developed her love of reading at a young age thanks to her fifth-grade teachers reading *Percy Jackson* during study hall, and she has never been the same since. Her favorite genres to edit are romance, fantasy, and science-fiction. As a former drum major of five years, she is also the communications director for The Drum Major Society, a 501(c)3 non-profit dedicated to the education and support of high school and college field commanders. When she isn't reading or editing, you can find Isabelle riding roller coasters, dancing, taking pictures of her cats, watching movies, or going to football games. Go Cats! and Go Blue!

D.A. SPRUZEN
The Turkish Connection
The Witch of Tut

J.M. PAQUETTE
Klauden's Ring
Solyn's Body
The Inbetween
Hannah's Heart

KYLE SORRELL
Munderworld
Potarium

LOU KEMP
The Violins Played Before Junstan
Music Shall Untune the Sky
The Raven and the Pig
The Pirate Danced and the Automat Died
The Wyvern, the Pirate, and the Madman

MEGAN MACKIE
Silverblood Scion

R.J. YOUNG
Challenges of Tawa
Witch of the Whirlwind

SYDNEY WILDER
Daughter of Serpents

VALERIE WILLIS
Cedric: The Demonic Knight
Romasanta: Father of Werewolves
The Oracle: Keeper of the Gaea's Gate
Artemis: Eye of Gaea
King Incubus: A New Reign

PARANORMAL & URBAN FANTASY

AMANDA FASCIANO
Waking Up Dead
Dead Vessel
Dead Show
Dead Revelations

BEAU LAKE
The Beast Beside Me
The Beast Within Me
Taming the Beast: Novella
The Beast After Me
Charming the Beast
The Beast Like Me
An Eye for Emeralds
Swimming in Sapphires
Pining for Pearls

CHELSEA BURTON DUNN
By Moonlight
Moon Bound

J.M. PAQUETTE
Call Me Forth
Invite Me In
Keep Me Close

KAIT DISNEY-LEUGERS
Antique Magic
Blood Magic
Heart Magic

LYRA R. SAENZ
Prelude
Falsetto in the Woods: Novella
Ragtime Swing
Sonata
Song of the Sea
The Devil's Trill
Bercuese
To Heal a Songbird
Ghost March
Nocturne

MARIA DEVIVO
Aestrangel the Fallen
Aestrangel the Chosen
Aestrangel the Risen

MEGAN MACKIE
The Saint of Liars
The Devil's Day
The Finder of the Lucky Devil

PAIGE LAVOIE
I'm in Love with Mothman
I'm Engaged to Mothman

ROBERT J. LEWIS
Shadow Guardian and the Three Bears
Shadow Guardian and the Big Bad Wolf
Shadow Guardian and the Boys
That Went Woof

www.ingramcontent.com/pod-product-compliance
Lightning Source LLC
Chambersburg PA
CBHW031546310726
48971CB00008B/2642